SWCAPA

ANTHOLOGY

At the Plumb Library

Connecticut Autors & Publishers Association.
Avon CT

SWCAPA Anthology
Copyright © 2018 by SW CAPA
(Southwest CT Authors & Publishers Assn.)

For information:

Joseph Keeney jkeeney9267@charter.net
Richard Colon richcolon_sr@yahoo.com

Dedication

To the Plumb Library Branch of Shelton, CT

Acknowledgment

Thank you to Plumb Library Coordinator Bob Anteramian for making our meetings possible. And, a thank you to SW-CAPA Director Joe Keeney and SW-CAPA Coordinator Rich Colon for making this book a reality. A special thanks to the Connecticut Authors & Publisher's without which the South West chapter would not exist.

Table of Contents

Preface

Connecticut Authors and Publishers Association (CAPA) was founded 20 years ago to help people who aspired to be published authors gain the necessay writing skills to accomplish their goals. In order to maintain that mission, CAPA offers its members mentoring, workshops and a speaker each month who is knowledgeable in the craft of writing, publishing and marketing.

Members can belong to any of the four chapters that make-up CAPA:

CAPA CENTRAL
Sycamore Hills Park Community Center, Avon, CT; Meet third Saturday of each month 10:30 am -- 12:30 pm
http://www.aboutcapa.com

CAPA SOUTHEAST
Groton Regency, 1145 Paquonnock Road, Route 1, Groton, CT; Meet third Monday of each Month; 6:30 pm
santostom@comcast.net

CAPA SOUTHWEST
Plumb Memorial Library, Shelton, CT. Meet 2nd Monday of each month.6:30 pm; jkeeney9267@charter.net

CAPA NORTHEAST
Willington Public Library, 7 Ruby Road, Willington, CT; Meet the first Saturday of each Month; 10:30 am felix@jbnovels.com

A professional writer is an amateur who didn't quit.

~ Richard Bach

Richard Colon

A Hard Life

Richard Colon

A small trickle of blood ran down the side of Robby's face; a second later and another bare-knuckled punch also left its' mark. This was not a professional boxing match; this was an inner-city street corner and a group of kids had crowded around to watch what appeared to be a helpless 14-year old boy lying on the ground getting badly beaten by a young man who is older and much stronger. However, Robby was the one who had started the fight (as usual) and he was far from helpless. While fighting is a common occurrence for Robby, it's not often that he is the one knocked down and getting bloodied.

Most people mistakenly believe that the person who is strongest and can inflict the most pain wins the fight. But more often than not, it is the person with the most stamina and who can endure the most pain that ultimately wins. Robby excelled at both. Whenever he finds himself in a difficult fight, Robby has the ability to put himself into a trance-like state, so that he doesn't feel the pain. While pinned to the ground, lying on his back, he analyzes his opponent's every move. Are the punches coming stronger from the right or from the left? Does his opponent seem to favor or protect any one part of his body more than another? Are there signs of fatigue? Or maybe overconfidence, thinking that Robby had no fight left in him. These are all weaknesses that can be exploited by a seasoned fighter, and despite his young age, Robby is seasoned.

As the fight continued, Robby carefully calculated his options and waited for the right moment. Another fist started coming down, and this time Robby smiled. He turned and shifted just enough so that the blow landed on the side of his head. He knows that the human skull is harder than the hand, and while not pleasant for Robby, it was actually more painful to the person throwing the punch. There was a slight pop and cracking sound, which Robby knew wasn't from his head, it was from the other guy's hand. His opponent was tired and in pain; this was the opportune moment that Robby had been waiting for.

The transformation was remarkable. Robby is lying on his back, no expression on his face. His breathing had slowed down and took on a focused rhythm. He grabbed his opponent's forearm and pulled down hard, which slammed the already swollen hand into the sidewalk. The resulting screams indicated that the hand was definitely broken. But that was just the beginning of the punishment that Robby had in mind. The roles were reversed, with Robby in charge, and he doesn't believe in showing any mercy. Earlier in the fight, he had noticed his opponent protecting his right side, maybe due to a previous injury. So Robby made certain that he punched hard on the right side, over and over again. Breaking a few ribs is a sure way to take the fight out of someone. And it was not long before no sounds or movement came from his opponent, who was sprawled on the sidewalk unconscious. But Robby didn't stop right away, he continued to hit again and again. Only stopping when he was satisfied that he would be the only one to stand and walk away.

Those in the crowd who were from the neighborhood knew to quickly make room and let Robby walkthrough. They remember a time when someone jumped Robby, just after he had finished a tough fight; thinking that it should be easy to beat him. Unfortunately for them, that way of thinking proved to be wrong. Robby fought even stronger and more vicious during that second fight, which ended with him as the last one standing and using his steel-toed boots to continually kick his attacker. When he was done, he had calmly asked who's next. There were no other challengers.

It was a short walk down the garbage-filled street and around the block to Robby's decaying apartment building. Once inside the hallway, he started brushing the dirt off his clothes as he climbed up the old worn stairs. At that moment, a figure appeared at the top of the landing. Robby slowly raised his head and looked up the dimly lit staircase to see a familiar image. The light shining down from behind the figure, cast a dark and eerie shadow.

"Well, you no good little bastard. Where have you been?"

Robby held his head down as he spoke, "Sorry Dad. Something came up."

His father was not a tall man, actually, he was shorter than Robby, but he was a large man. Looming at the top of the stairs, the shadowy silhouette looked even more ominous because of the crutches.

"Something came up? Is that your excuse? I don't give a damn what happened as long as you got my cigarettes."

Polio is a devastating disease and had taken a toll on the man physically, mentally, and emotionally. Maybe that was his excuse for being an alcoholic, but he was not just a drunk, he was what they call a mean drunk.

"Um, Dad. I um... didn't get the cigs. I'm sorry."

"You're sorry? You're sorry? Being sorry ain't gonna get me my smokes."

Robby continued his climb up to the top of the stairs, accepting the inevitable. His father continued to berate him.

"A good for nothing loser, that's what you are. You can't do anything right. What have you been doing? You've been fighting again, haven't you? Didn't that special school straighten you out."

The 'special' school was actually a reformatory school for boys, which is just a polite name for a youth prison, which was situated on an old country farm. The school never really straightened out any of the boys that were sent there. Instead, they left with more anger and hatred than when they arrived. What did anyone expect would happen, when you mix boys who went in for truancy with boys who have committed armed robbery and assault? The school also taught some hard lessons about survival. For example, even though the grounds had minimum security, there was rarely a successful escape. Because the main deterrent was a policy whereby if a boy was trying to run away, other boys were sent out to track him down. And whoever caught the runner, would earn a free weekend pass to go home, along with other special perks. The scene was reminiscent of a pack of wolves hunting down their prey, with almost the same fateful conclusion. One of the school hunting parties had ended badly when Robby had tried to escape and was confronted by a group of boys who cornered him inside a barn. The school covered up the incident, which resulted in a serious injury with one of the boys being stabbed with a pitchfork. From this environment, Robby learned quite a few lessons, none of which would make him a better person.

"So you want a fight, well I'll give you a good one!" shouted his father.

Just as Robby reached the top step, he was slammed against the wall. One crutch was pressed hard against his stomach, the other held across his throat. Through all the pain, Robby never said a word or even made a sound; he just stared at his father.

"All this fighting and street hoodlum crap is just a game to you, isn't it? Well, my boy, we can play our game, can't we?"

While his father was considered to be disabled, he was far from being weak, and his upper body was amazingly strong. He easily lifted Robby up and pushed him into the living room where they stood facing each other. From behind his back, Robby's father pulled out an old and battered revolver. He opened the cylinder and emptied the rounds onto the floor, except for one that he kept in his hand. He held it up to show Robby, then he slowly and methodically put the round into one of the empty chambers. With a flip of his wrist, the gun snapped closed. As he spun the cylinder of the .38 special, he flashed a sinister grin. He raised the gun and held it straight out. Robby felt the cold steel barrel pressed firmly against the center of his forehead. Silent and showing no sign of emotion, Robby held his ground and stared right back at his father.

As the trigger was slowly pulled, the cylinder turned and the hammer was drawn back. The sound seemed deafening as the hammer came crashing down, but was merely a click since it fell on an empty chamber. Father and son, they both stood motionless not knowing who should move first. Finally, Robby backed away. The circular indentation from the gun barrel was clearly visible on his skin.

Without a word, Robby turned around and slowly walked toward his room. He then stopped to look back at his father who was standing with a crutch under one arm, his other arm outstretched and still holding the gun. His father's hair was damp, as sweat was dripping down his face; his breathing was heavy and labored and the hand holding the gun started to visibly shake. They stared at each other in silence with the quivering gun still pointed across the room at Robby. In a soft tender voice, Robby spoke, "Don't worry Dad. Someday we will both get our wish."

His father did not move nor speak as he held back the tears. Robby closed the door to his room, shut off the light, and went to bed. He welcomed the escape that sleep would bring.

The Dancer

Richard Colon

Clara was the owner of a struggling pet shop in Talisport Maine. She was happy that she had picked-up her life and moved to the quant little town, but it has not been easy. Clara was not a local and would never be considered as one, especially due to the gossip and half-truths that spread as easily as the wind.

The whispered rumors going around the town, was that Clara was a dancer when she lived in New York city; a pole dancer at a sleazy nightclub. To be honest, part of it was true, she was a dancer, but she was by far not a pole dancer. But some people didn't care about the truth, and for the longest time she was treated as the town leper.

Some degree of acceptance finally occurred, but it only started after that one memorable event. It was the fall festival, and the mayor had invited the Governor and his wife to the opening ceremonies. Everyone was surprised at the Governor's acceptance to attend, even the mayor.

For New England, it was a perfect autumn day, with all the leaves having turned from green to bright orange and crimson. There were many speeches by the town officials and the Governor. But it was the governor's wife who changed everything for Clara. At the microphone, as she addressed the crowds, she spoke about all the great things they have to be proud of in Talisport. And she ended her remarks with a reminder, that they should be especially proud to have such a famous and talented citizen living in their town. The wonderful Clara Jennings who had retired from the New York City Ballet.

To some of the locals, it made a big impression, but others thought that it must be a mistake. After all, Clara was just some pole dancer.

Your Hand in Mine

Richard Colon

When we were young our hands fit together;
at first soft, tender, and sensuous

As the years passed they became firm,
strong, and supportive

Now as we move on, they have started to become
more
slight, weathered, and frail

But our hands still fit together;
the decades have molded them into a perfect match

One would be lost without the other

Derek Coutouras

A Fortune Told

Derek Couturas

It was 1918 the fourth year of the Great War. Thousands of young men had perished in the fields of Belgium, fighting in the conflict between Kaiser Wilhelm's armies and the forces of England and France. Now the United States of America was taking a hand, so called "doughboys" the soldiers of General Jack Pershing's army had arrived. They thronged the Channel ports, brash young men impatiently waiting to "go over" and prove their mettle.

Fortune telling was Carla's livelihood. She traveled with the carnival working the Channel ports. For one silver shilling she would reveal a client's future, and before they left her presence she would astound them further, revealing a hidden detail of their past. At each stop she would make ready, erecting her little canvas booth. For herself she would tie up her shining black tresses with a mystical kerchief and adorn herself with beaded necklaces. She lived and traveled in a little horse drawn caravan inherited from her Romany father. She could barely remember her mother; she had died when Carla was a little child.

Before she turned eighteen, Carla took a husband. Their joining celebrated to the brassy lilt of concertinas and the declaration of toasts in brewed beer. But in the way of the Romany her man soon strayed, eventually gone forever. As time passed there were more partners but none blossomed into a lasting relationship. The longest was three years, the shortest three days.

Eventually her only companion was a haughty Siamese cat that had moved in with her soon after her last paramour disappeared. She named her Sheba to which the Siamese responded with typical feline condescension.

Before the outbreak of war, the patrons of Carla's booth were mostly women, desiring to know the future of romantic liaisons. Would they marry? How many offspring would they have? But as the war advanced young soldiers stopped by. They sought to look into the window of an uncertain future, hoping for a mystic confirmation that they would outlive the war. Sitting on the edge of a chair opposite her, they would mask their anxiety, pretending that it was all just a lark, but wanting to know – "Will I survive"?

As the conflict wore on the Americans arrived. They caroused in the pubs and frequented the carnival, as the British soldiers had, that went before them.

In order to 'see,' receive a vision, Carla had to touch her clients physically. Therefore, she simulated reading their palms, their hand resting in hers. Equally, the large crystal that sat on the low table before her, alternately clouding and sparkling, yielded nothing, it was no more than a charismatic prop. She was often shaken by the terrible revelations aroused in her seeing. Abruptly she would withdraw her hand, steeling herself not to shudder, struggling to maintain a countenance of calm. Emotionally unable to convey a picture of the destruction and death to which a young soldier was condemned, she would soften her telling,

"Soon you will have difficulties in your life, but with the fortitude given to you, by the family that raised you, and the bravery that I see within you, you will overcome. Your blessing will one day be a good life with a wife and children."

They would leave, thoughtful, somewhat reassured.

One cold afternoon a young man appeared, stooping into the entrance of Carla's booth. His uniform along with his high crowned hat betrayed that he was an American waiting to go over. He stood before her, his build slight, still growing into manhood. He stammered under the gaze of Carla's almond eyes.

"Will you. Will you tell my fortune?"

"Please be seated," invited Carla, gesturing toward the opposite chair.

He fumbled in his pocket for a shilling, dropping it into the green bowl at her elbow.

Carla arose and drew a heavy black drape decorated with silver half-moons and occult signs across the doorway.

Although she had seen many like him, Carla was drawn to this young man. He looked at her, his adolescent face fresh and earnest, his pale eyes worried but brave. Carla sat quickly, her ankles had turned to water. She became aware that she was no longer in command of the séance, her hands fluttered as she took the felt cover off the crystal ball. Sheba stole from beneath the table, arching her spine along his ankle, purring her approval.

"Show me your palm." Her mouth felt dry, He pushed back the right cuff of his uniform extending his arm across the table. She slid her brown hand beneath his, her long fingers curling and holding it. Her throat grew tight.

"The other," she gasped. He extended his left arm, palm toward the ceiling, she grasped his hand with her right, again her fingers curled and held. Her eyes closed, her shoulders quivered.

"You are Bobby, your mother is French, and you are from a place called Maine. Your father traps lobsters. He is from the people that always lived in Maine. Your mother is silent."

"By thunder you're good," burst out the young soldier. "I am Bobby, my father is descended from the Native Americans, and my mother is a mute." His voice fell as he uttered the last phrase.

"For your mother I am sorry, it happened a long time ago, she was good to you, always. So was your father," replied Carla opening her eyes.

"My mother?" questioned Bobby.

"The words will come back to her one day. It will be before you grow old, and before your father stops lobstering because of the rheumatism."

"That would be a wonderful thing," Bobby's eyes looked into hers across the crystal ball.

"My company goes over in two weeks"? She knew his question.

"You will return here where I am." She further added words of romance, stated in Romany.

Since this young man had stood before her, she had seen much. Her world had moved. For Carla a new life had begun. She unclasped her hands and pushed them into the folds of her flowing black dress.

"Yes here. This I know. I cannot tell you more now. The other was the Romany of long ago, only for you." She unhooked the black drape letting it fall away. "You must go now. Come back tomorrow, Sunday, everything will be closed. We will have tea and I will read the leaves."

Puzzled, he said, "I don't know if I can."

She took his hand, "I know that you can. You will come. The blue caravan behind the booth.

Carla ushered him through the door and re-hung the black drape.

He returned the next day, smart in his best uniform.

"The army had a church parade this morning; my company had to march around the park. But we were dismissed after the service, so I came here right away." He was awkward, embarrassed to stand at the door of her caravan under the gaze of passing fairground people. She drew him inside. On the little woodstove oat cakes cooked in a round pan, sharing the hot surface with an iron teapot.

"You are here Bobby, it cannot be any other way," She moved close to him and unbuttoned his tunic coat, sliding it off his shoulders and laying it on the brass bed in the corner. "Thank you for inviting me Carla," he said, still a little awkward as she handed him an oat cake and poured tea into china cups.

"We will sit here," she said, indicating the bed where she had put his coat. There was only one chair, an old rocker sitting in the middle of the felt carpet. Bobby drained his cup and stared in at the black mix of tealeaves.

"Can you read them?" He asked.

"Not so well as the palms," admitted Carla. "But enough to see that we will both be happy from here on."

She took his free hand and held it to her lips and then quickly placed her other hand behind his head, drawing his lips to hers. He returned her kiss in an explosion of passion, abandoning himself to the moment. The empty cup thudded onto the floor. He dragged her closer, like a drowning man grasping at life.

"I love you," he gasped.

"We will always love each other," she murmured.

"Are we going to....? I mean I've never done....

There was a crash on the door followed by a thunderous hammering. The door flew open, a USA army sergeant stood on the threshold, two military policemen behind him.

"Come on son you'll have to do this on another day," He drawled. "Orders to move, we're rounding up the whole company. We'll be in France by this time tomorrow."

Bobby shrugged into his tunic. "Hurry it up," growled the sergeant. Carla opened a little inlaid box and produced a brass key. Calmly she whispered, "Keep this, it will protect you always, never be without it." She slid it into the pocket of his tunic.

"Quick march," ordered the sergeant. She watched as the little party marched away, joining a larger assemblage on the perimeter of the fairground.

Carla kept on telling fortunes, moving as

before from town to town with the carnival. She was kind as always, skirting around any tragedy that she saw in a patron's future.

Six months to the day that Bobby had been marched away, she cleaned her caravan, prepared oat cakes, filled the teapot with fresh water and sprinkled tea leaves into it. Then she put clean sheets on the brass bed, took off her shoes and padded over to a corner niche. From behind a brocade curtain she produced a gossamer black negligee. She shook it out and laid it on the bed. Smiling, she took off all her clothes and slid into the black negligee. Finally, she removed the kerchief from her head, allowing her long black hair to fall about her shoulders.

She stretched back on the clean sheets, torrid, anticipating. Beneath the bed Sheba purred tuning to her mistress' languor. The door to her Bardolph eased open.

A figure stood there, hesitating.

"Bobby."

"Carla. I've, brought back the key," he answered.

She held out her arms, "Come with me, it is our time."

Awkwardly he stepped forward; his face, once fresh with youth now lined and pinched.

A pair of crutches flanked his remaining leg. The empty trouser leg, where once there had been a whole limb, pinned up to prevent it from dragging.

"I'm not the same," his voice was low, full of regret. "I couldn't ask you to... to love me."

Carla arose from the bed, her voice thick with passion, "I've waited for you my love, I knew, I saw it from the beginning. I love you Bobby."

She took the crutches and cast them aside,

supporting him on his good leg, his arm across her shoulders. He sank onto the bed, tears running down his cheeks. She kissed him tenderly, murmuring soft Romany words. First, she removed his tunic and vest and then kneeling, carefully removed his trousers and underclothes.

He lay back; she folded into his body, careful not to harm his stump.

"No one can separate us now, we are one."

The Price of Valor

Derek Couturas

Martin and Donald lived and grew up in the little lumber township of St Mare. Their homes were the spare frame houses built to house the working families of Northern Maine. Martin's family, the 'De Boufs' were of French Canadian extraction and had moved down from Quebec a generation ago. They too settled into a home on the same dirt street as Donald's family, the Smiths.

Donald's family roots went back to before the "Great Depression" when St Mare was no more than a steam driven sawmill with a collection of raw stick houses grouped around it.

Being of the same age and physique the two boys formed a strong attachment. They supported each other in school yard confrontations, struggled with homework together. Played Little League on the same team exalting in the teams' wins and commiserating with each other when they lost. The two boys' close friendship created a warm association between the two families. It was an association of respect and friendship that stayed strong throughout their school years.

The war in Indo-China seemed far away from the little community of St Mare. People took little notice, seeing the conflict as an Asian problem. However, it soon became apparent that America was taking part. The ideaolgy of Communism in the Vietnamese peninsula was unacceptable to the United States. As the war escalated more troops were needed. Eventually the Draft was instituted.

Martin and Donald graduated from St Mare High School the same year that the Draft lottery came into being. Their families were staggered when the two boys, now young adults, received draft notices. They were both ordered to report to Fort Bragg for basic training.

The horror of the Vietnam conflict had been playing out in graphic detail over the news media for the past few years. The expected quick ending had reversed into a deepening war with no end in sight. The Smith family were somewhat sober, but obviously proud. Donald could not contain the elation and sense of purpose that the draft notice gave him. His father had served in World War II and brought home a medal. His grandfather had served in WW1. He was young and strong and more than ready to serve, as his father and grandfather had before him.

His friend Martin, did not exhibit the same excitement. When Donald rushed into the De Bouf's kitchen waving his draft notice the whole family were seated around the table wearing glum expressions. "I've been drafted," he blurted.

"Hello Donald, so has Martin," replied Mrs. De Bouf. There were tears in her eyes and she looked fearful. Mr. De Bouf sat at the table staring straight ahead, his face a black cloud of anger. Martin pushed back from the table and said, "Let's go into the yard." Donald followed him outside. They perched on an old garden swing, Martin saying nothing.

"I'll bet, that if we report together, we'll be put in the same outfit," exclaimed Donald. "And I've got an idea. Let's both go down to the Marine recruiting office and volunteer. Wouldn't it be great to be Marines?"

Martin's reply did not reflect his friend's enthusiasm, "I don't know Donnie, I'm not sure that I want to go to war. Look at the TV. There is a whole lot of misery going on over there."

Donald gestured with his draft notice. "We don't have a choice. Come on Marty let's try for the Marines. We're both great athletes, we're the kind of guys the Marines are looking for. And besides, the uniforms are really neat, the girls will love us."

Martin, shuffled his feet and then, looking directly at his friend, replied, "I'm not going."

"C'mon, the army is dull let's try for the Marines."

"I mean that I'm not going for any of it. It's wrong."

"Okay then, we'll go for the Army. Let's try to stay together."

"You're not listening to me Donnie. I'm not going, that's it."

"You scared? It's okay to be scared."

"The hell with you Donnie. I'm not scared."

"You sound scared. You're even starting to smell scared."

They both came to their feet and stood facing each other their fists clenched. The screen door banged open. Martin's father made his way over to the swing. He stared at the two young men facing each other, their faces flushed, their eyes wild. He spoke to Donald, "Donald would you mind going over to your house and give your parents a message.

"Sure Mr. Le Beouf," replied Donald, not taking his eyes of Martin.

"Ask them if they wouldn't mind coming over for a cup of coffee. Martin's mother and I would like to talk to them about the draft notices you boys have received." Without answering Donald strode away in the direction of his own house.

Minutes later he returned with his mother and father. Both families seated themselves at the kitchen table. Mrs. Le Bouf offered coffee but everyone declined.

"About the draft notices," began Mr. Le Bouf. "Martin is going to take a trip to Canada. We have family there and he's going to stay with them. We could probably make arrangements for Donald to go with him. He could stay there as well."

"There's no time for trips they have to be at the draft board office within two days," replied Mr. Smith.

Mrs. Le Bouf spoke, "We're not planning on Martin coming back for some time."

The Smiths didn't speak. They just directed their gaze onto Martin. "You're 'gonna' run, Martin?" Mr. Smith's question was blunt, spoken to hit home.

His voice high with emotion Martin replied, "It's a bad war. It's a killing of peasants and children and I don't want to live with that the rest of my life."

Mr. Smith blurted, "You're running. It's the duty of every good American in the time of war to serve, not hide."

Mrs. Smith chimed in, her voice sour, "You're

a coward Martin." To his parents she said, "You should march him down to the draft office and make sure he signs up."

Martin's mother responded, "My boy's no coward, it takes courage to do what he is doing."

Donald spoke, his voice echoing his mother's bitterness, "Don't worry, any of you, I'll do it for both of us. I'm not yellow." Mr. Le Bouf arose from the table, strode to the door and threw it open.

"Leave at once," he ordered. Mrs. Smith preceded her husband through the door. "This is a coward house I'm glad to go," she commented

Donald paused with his hand on the screen door and looked back at his old friend and then followed his parents.

"Don't ever cross my threshold again," yelled Mrs. Le Bouf to their departing backs.

Nine months later young Donald Smith returned. His casket was shipped home to St Mare. The little lumber town in Northern Main, where he grew up. His family wanted it that way. "I want Donnie near us," said his mother. There was a letter from his commanding officer, telling of Donald's bravery under fire. President Johnson sent a letter of regret and gratitude for Donnie's service along with a flag.

The Le Boufs made no recognition of Donald's return. Their son, Donald's one-time friend, stayed in Canada. He never came back. Not even after President Carter pardoned all the Draft Dodgers in January 1977.

The two families continued living and working in St Mare. They never spoke to each other again.

Dave Gregory

A Little Piece of Leather

Dave Gregory

(6/23/18)
In the trunk of the car
In the back of the closet
In the back of my mind
There is a little piece of leather —

It was a birthday gift
Or a young studied purchase
With rawhide to tighten and chew
Holding together that little piece of leather —

Soon it was making fantastic plays
In the backyard stadium
To the cheers of a crowd of one
Flashing that wonderful little piece of leather —

A life full of endless summers
It went to neighborhood games
It tried to make the Little League team
That little piece of leather —

Still its most important role in life
Was what the players struggled to say
Groundballs and pop-ups thrown
Teaching, learning, how to use that little piece of
leather —

The ball goes from one glove to the other
"I love you Dad" — "I love you Son"
"I love you Dad" — "I love you Daughter"
The slap of the ball hitting that little piece of
leather —

I am as good as I can be
I am proud of all that you are
The volumes spoken
By a little piece of leather —

Lonesome Sailor

Dave Gregory
(5/5/18 & 5/26/18)

He ran away.
Away from nothing,
A life that was failing him.
There was no love.
Punished for being at the table
Taking up valuable space —

He first just ran.
Away from the house — the town
When he stopped
He was alone.
Barely in his teens
There was no master plan —

First there was survival.
How to eat and stay warm —
But, there had to be more.
What was going to have meaning?

Not just, what would he do tomorrow.
No, he needed more —

That night, hidden from sight
He felt safe and slept.
And for the first time in a long time, he dreamed.
The next morning, he held onto the dream.
Now, he headed toward something.
Determined, stepping lively, he was moving —

Walking along the side of the road,
Getting a ride in a wagon,
Working for meals and a few coins,
Heading east, always east.
Each hill spilled into a valley,
It seemed never ending —

Finally, he came upon another hill to climb.
But, now his footsteps quickened.
Weariness fell from his ragged shoes.
He was climbing and he could smell it.
At the top of the hill, it laid before him,
As far as he could see — the ocean — the sea —

Down the hill, through the seaport town,
To the docks, the smells, the chaos.
Ships headed down the coast,
Ships bringing goods across the ocean,
Ships setting out to catch fish, whales.
Ships! Ships, rigging, crates, owners and sailors —

He was drunk with awe and happiness.
One of these ships would be his home.
Whatever had to be done would be done.
At first he was pushed away or ignored.

But this was his time, now, no stopping him.
Finally, he found her; the Cathy Anne —

She was a rather small ship.
She was a rather old ship.
She was not in good repair.
Still her masts were tall and straight
And those walking her decks seemed content.
He presented himself at a table at the foot of the
gangplank —

With a boldness beyond his years,
Strengthened by the miles he's traveled,
He asked for a job on the Cathy Anne.
The three men sitting at the table paid him no
mind,
They were talking business, and the boy didn't
exist.
Near tears he slammed his fists on the table —

The three heads turned and looked at him.
With all the hate and frustration inside,
The boy again asked for a job on "his" ship.
Smiles came down on him, "your" ship?
Yes, I've come a long distance
And it was this ship that called me —

What about your parents?
Do they know you are here?
Do they know you've come to "your" ship?
They don't care and I'll work hard.
These three men kept their smiles.
We do need a cabin boy, interested? —

They would pay him for doing what he wanted.
Yes, he would learn what to do.
Yes, he understood it was hard work.
Yes, he knew he would be at sea a long time.
He made his mark — he was ready,
He was a member of the crew of the Cathy Anne —

And so it began, this life of a lonesome sailor.
The following morning, on the high tide
The Cathy Anne set to sea with a full cargo.
She was headed for the Bahamas,
There she would sell her goods
And then take on a new load and bring it to a new
port —

A cabin boy was the lowest of the low.
There was no one lower on the ship.
The captain was a fair and patient man.
He taught his crew how to work together
And explained, to those who didn't know,
What he expected from them —

The cabin boy got his sea legs quickly.
Learned what was expected and did it.
He fetched, delivered, and cleaned, all of that.
Always the one on call and proving himself reliable.
When he was able, he listened to the old timers,
He absorbed the salt from their stories and carried
on. —

When they reached port, he hung close to the ship.
After a time, he found his voice and asked
questions.
The butt of a joke or two, he handled it well.

The crew accepted him and took him under their
wing.
Most spoke kindly to him
And more importantly, some befriended him. —

As the ship moved on, port to port,
He took on more responsibility
And seemed to have a natural calling.
With the hard work, came physical fitness.
With the friendships, came knowledge.
Never had he had such a wonderful education. —

Days flew and months matured him.
Now a year and no dirt crossed his path.
With care, he expanded his world.
He ventured into towns he had never heard of,
Streets in ports around the world
And his knowledge and seamanship grew. —

It was more than two years at sea
Before the Cathy Anne returned to her homeport.
The lonesome sailor strode down the gangplank.
He was almost unrecognizable to the three owners.
They sat at their table and greeted each member of
the crew,
Handing them their shares, for a job well done. —

Some nodded and walked off, never to return,
Others signed on for another tour.
One of the owners asked the cabin boy:
How was your time at sea?
How were the adventures on "your" ship?
Would you like to sail on the Cathy Anne again? —

Aye, I would like to sail with her.

To feel the breeze in my face at dawn time
Or study the stars during the night watch.
Smell the water and hear the ship.
The Cathy Anne talks to me, she believes in me,
But, I'll not go again as a cabin boy. —

The owners nodded their understanding.
None had ever been a sailor.
They spent their lives in banks and offices,
Still they knew the value of a good man.
The captain had already talked to them.
Here was the newest sailor on the Cathy Anne. —

Off again and off again on the high tide,
Full cargo, weather fair, weather foul.
Learning his trade, doing what was asked and
more.
Listening to the old-timers, heeding their advice.
Working hard, with no complaints.
Still a loner though, thoughts quiet inside him. —

Now an old hand, he had his chances to move on.
But he loved the Cathy Anne and she loved him.
They were flawed, but their love grew strong.
His craft strengthened still, he moved up the ranks.
Eventually an officer, leadership by example
Harsh words, only to be heard above a storm —

Only once was he unhappy on his ship.
Needing a cargo out of Cuba,
They took on a short run to Charleston.
There were no crates to be lifted onto the decks.
No sacks to be lowered into the hold.
This cargo walked aboard and smelled of fear. —

Off-loaded from a big ship out of Africa,
These were people of flesh and bone.
Men, women, children, pushed into the hold,
So many cattle to be delivered, to be sold.
He understood their language, but not their words.
And those in charge of them, held his disgust. —

It was hard for him to understand someone missing
home.
Their skin color was darker than his own-
sunburned complexion,
But, he never missed where he came from.
He was lonesome perhaps, but now a loner too.
His ship was his family, each board, each hank of
rope,
No tender flesh walked a widow's walk for him. —

With the cargo put ashore in Charleston,
He waited for what would come next.
For the first time, he thought of leaving the Cathy
Anne.
But, cotton was loaded, on its way to England.
No more cries of anguish, just cries to set sail,
To haul away, to pull up anchor, to sail on the high
tide. —

Comfortable climbing the rigging, securing the
cargo,
Enduring the storms and the doldrums,
Our sailor, our officer moved across the world.
Faces changed, new men, he learned from them all.
What not to do from some, what to do from most,
And he never missed, what he never had. —

His world covered the wide world,
But his world was quite small.
Judged only by how it affected him and the Cathy
Anne,
He walked her weathered decks,
Looking only to judge their condition
And make repairs as were needed. —

Never on the land for very long,
He distrusted things on shore.
The docks were rough, full of danger.
Protecting his few worldly possessions,
Always the observer, watching, learning,
He might sip a drink, but was always sober. —

Yes, he had sampled church going,
Listening to the preacher's fire and brimstone.
Yes, he had sampled the ladies of the night,
But few wanted to talk of life.
When the ship was ready to set sail,
He was ready to cast off to a new port. —

His eyes watched the heavens,
Studying what God and nature
Would have in store for him.
Carving small pieces of wood to pass the time,
Or reading a book about life at sea
To improve his abilities as a sailor. —

Then came the crossing, the last crossing.
He was at middle age for that age,
Feeling some aches and pains without working for
them.
The dawn never came and the night disappeared,
And a great gray surrounded them.

Waves became restless and the wind took over. —

All hands were called on deck to make ready.
A storm had caught them and wasn't letting go.
Ropes were rigged to be held when needed.
Cargo tied down, hatches secured,
Everything was made ready.
The battle lines drawn, the troops were engaged. —

Keeping the ship into the wind
Became the primary chore.
Waves now towered over the Cathy Anne,
Crashing head on, or washing sideways across the
deck.
Lightning joined in the battle with pelting rain.
The ship was lifted high, like a feather, and then
dropped like a brick. —

The crew pumped water out from below decks,
As they dodged crates torn free.
A bolt from Zeus split the main mast and toppled it.
Man overboard! The wheel spun freely,
No two men could hold her steady.
Darkness climbed into the thoughts of all aboard.

The lonesome sailor did all he knew how,
But it did no good, he was out numbered.
Each wave took its toll on the Cathy Anne.
Her heart was ripped away in pieces
And so too that of the crew.
She broke apart in the middle of the North
Atlantic. —

When the sky cleared and the waters calmed,
There was life only under the sea.

Hardy men had been dragged below the surface,
Nothing will ever reach the shore.
But never fear, the love affair continues,
Between the Cathy Anne and her lonesome sailor.

Photos on the Piano

Dave Gregory
(11/23/16)

When you walk by the old house on the corner
Beyond the well kept hedge and rose trellis
You can see into the parlor window
Just beyond the glass is a piano
On the piano sits a large group of framed photos

When invited in, you gather in the parlor
The piano dominates a very old-fashioned room

Where the rest of the house is rather up to date
This room has been frozen in time, a museum
Those photos, backed by the sunlight
Draw you to them as they sit on a crocheted runner

→

A well-aged picture of a couple catches your eye
He is stiff and uncomfortable in his "formal" clothes
She has a smile of complete happiness in her
wedding dress
He would go on to build this house
She would add the warmth and comfort

The rest of the photos descend from this one
The little girl for whom the piano was bought
Smiles at you from the yard with her dog
Ignoring her piano lessons and chores

Through the generations, frozen in time
We see other couples and children
Grandchildren, brothers, sisters, aunts and uncles

The assorted frames cover several lifetimes
Some near works of art, others casual snapshots
But they all portray happiness and delight

You have not intruded, but were welcomed guests
By the current smiling occupants
Descendants of the builder and his wife
Welcomed with warmth and comfort
Of all those framed residents and friends
Who watch from photos on the piano

Mike Hotchkiss

Jailbreak!

Mike Hotchkiss

Amanda, Pete and Rob were new to the jailbreaking business. If Rob had not been wrongly convicted of assault, none of them would have ever thought of orchestrating one. College degrees and well-paying jobs did not a conspiracy to commit a felony make.

They were three months in the planning and a few hours from executing a plan to break Rob out of the Cheshire Correctional Facility, a medium-security prison in the middle of Connecticut.

Amanda and Pete were sitting in a breakfast nook at their condo in Branford overlooking the Long Island Sound. Amanda had just poured them coffee and Pete was plucking grapes from a bowl while looking intently at a hand drawn map.

Amanda said, "Do you think we have estimated the blackout time properly? It makes me nervous that we only give Rob 15 seconds to get from the middle of the exercise yard to the fence."

"Unfortunately," replied Pete, "That is one of the many SWAGS we had to make. We had to guess the location of the guards on watch, etc. We are at the stage where we should focus on executing the plan, not second guessing our assumptions. There were a lot of assumptions in the *'Brinks Job'* too.

Amanda replied, "I know. It's just this is finally sinking in. We're breaking a felon from prison! It's not a damn movie, we're actually going to do this!"

Pete reached across the table and stroked his wife's hand. "Thanks for the coffee," he said, "We have to remind ourselves why this is necessary. Not the right thing to do, not a crusade, but something that **must** be done."

Amanda nodded and looked at the map. Pete was pointing to the northwest corner of the prison yard. This was where they had been able to dig a two-foot tunnel under the fence a mere six hours ago. She recalled, "I remember when you first thought of this and I thought you were batshit crazy. Now, I can't believe how easy it was to pull off. A few public records from the town hall and befriending one of the prison guards was all we needed to figure it out."

"Don't forget the tricky part of getting a two-way radio into Rob. The drone diversion you planned was brilliant!"

Grinning Amanda said, "Thanks, I guess being able to talk to Rob, was a critical part. I'm shocked that the inner fence is electrified but has no concrete foundation, while the outer fence has solid concrete under the perimeter but is not electrified."

"Yes," said Pete, "When this is over, 'they' will certainly question the design. A gap cut through the outer fence and a *'Great Escape'* tunnel dug under the inner. So simple a breach risk unnoticed for the 50-year history since the prison opened...just like *'Escape from Alcatraz'*.

"Love Steve McQueen," crowed Amanda.

"That's why I'm calling you 'Bullitt'!" Pete laughed.

They went back to discussing the plan details. Pete gained confidence as they've-reviewed the plan. Amanda was slow to dispel doubts. "The assumption..."

Pete cut her off, "Assumption. That word is banned from conversation until this is over. Capiche?"

"Capiche," she fake smiled.

~~~

Rob sat in his 10 x 10 cell and continued a running dialogue with himself. Skeptic Rob battled with Upbeat Rob:

Skeptic Rob:

God, I can't believe I'm going through with this. So many things can go wrong with the plan.

Upbeat Rob:

Just think about all the detailed planning. Pete and Amanda are the best.

SR:

It's not the confidence I have in my friends, it's all the assumptions. Yes, I was able to give them paced off dimensions and yes, I gave the recreation routine and schedule, but blacking out the prison and getting under one fence and through another in 15 seconds, is a stretch and the timeframe is, well, a complete guess!

UR:

It's a conservative estimate. If I were to call it a guess, I would use SWAG. Even without rehearsing you know it's only 60 feet of ground to cover. Remember breaking 12 seconds in the 100-yard sprint in school? This is only 20 easy yards.

He laughed at himself as he took a pace and spun around to represent each side of the discussion. *Prison may be getting to you,* thought Real Rob. He realized now was the time to rehearse the plan in his mind yet again.

UR:

Tonight, at rec break, do exactly as I have done for the last month. I will have the contraband radio on my person, so don't scratch my nuts. At the five-minute mark, I proceed to a spot in the northwest corner, ten paces from the fence facing inward. I hit the transmit button on the radio and hold it for five seconds. Pete and Amanda will know I'm ready.

After the power goes out, I pivot 180 degrees and run like hell to the spot. Find the dirt covered plank of wood, slide it aside and slither under the de-electrified fence. Turn 45 degrees to the north and run to the exterior fence where Pete will be with the fence spread open; the same gap they used the previous night to access the inner fence.

SR:

That's enough! You can leave out the final steps of darting to the large oak tree where two Vespas are hiding under sticks and leaves. Traversing an open field to Rte 10 where you make a turn into the alley near the clock tower and ride the Vespas up the ramp to an idling moving truck with Amanda in the driver's seat. Nothing could go wrong with this?

UR:

Dammit, I'm Andy Fucking Dufresne! I didn't even get to the part when the lights come on.

SR:

You don't have to. This should happen when Pete and I are almost to the Vespas. The search lights will come on automatically; protocol after an outage.

The prison guards will assume the worst but will not know what, who or where. We'll almost be to Rte 10 when they spot us. This is the part where Pete and I get shot from a sniper rifle.
UR:
*It's a **medium** security prison. Amanda told us they will not fire for any reason unless someone's life is in danger. She was confident of this as her new guard friend had told her.*
SR:
A lot of things I've been told about this is based on this friendship. I just hope he wasn't bullshitting her. I'm tired of thinking about it. Eight hours until show time. Ready?
Real Rob:
Ready!

~~~

Pete huddled next to the substation that feeds the prison. He had unearthed the junction box housing a simple switch he had installed less than a week ago. Pete was an electrician and knew things. Things like how easy it is to disconnect a 13kV High Voltage supply from a substation to a prison with a remote activated fuse. Pete had rigged the feed a few nights previous. Cheshire is a sleepy town, so a man with a hard hat poking around a substation at 3 am didn't attract attention. Plus, the station was off the main road, in a field, 60 yards from the northwest corner of the Cheshire Correctional Facility.

Pete adjusted the frequency and pressed the transmit button, "Bullitt, this is Basher" said with a bad British accent, "Are you in position?" He half whispered like a cop in a surveillance scene. They had given each other "handles" ostensibly to avoid interception. They liked movies and used characters that fit the roles in their real-life production. 'Banker' was Rob's character.

Bullitt replied, "I'm in the parking lot, ready to move to the alley."

Basher checked the time, 6:55 pm. "Proceed, Operation Monte Cristo starts in ten minutes. See you in the alley. Love my Bullitt!"

"Love you too Bash. See you in eleven minutes and 30 seconds. Oh, lose the bloody accent!"

~~~

Rob stood in the yard, ten-feet from the northwest corner, facing in. *Don't scratch your nuts!* He depressed the transmit button through the front of his prison-issued jumpsuit and held it for five seconds.

The lights in the yard went out. Rob's heart rate went up. The Banker turned around and ran. He didn't notice the ensuing commotion. He got to the fence and found the board on the first try – *holy shit!* It slid across the ground as he slinked under the de-electrified fence. *Andy Fuckin' Dufresne!*

He veered 45 degrees to the north and continued. His eyes had adjusted and he saw Pete's dark figure straight ahead with an open gap in the chain link fence.

Sirens came to life and the floodlights came on. The Banker was at the fence within touching distance of Basher when the voice bellowed "HALT!"

"CUT." The Director shouted. He moved forward with the stage crew applauding. "Great job guys"

"Do it just like that at the opening tonight and we've got ourselves a Broadway hit!

Love Unplugged

Michael Hotchkss

It was a perfect clock for me: unreliable, inaccurate. You could only see the numbers up close but didn't know if they were right. From afar, you couldn't see the numbers at all. I didn't want to know the time right now. It was a perfect clock.

It sat on my wife's bedside table and didn't make noise or it would cease to be perfect.

It allowed me to hear the sounds of the breeze rustling the autumn leaves beyond the open window. The fresh air had an aroma unique to the month of October in Vermont. Pamela and I loved the fall, loved Vermont and had made it a routine to spend time every autumn embedded in the enchantment of both. I bought her a gold encrusted maple leaf necklace on our first trip together, before we married. It came from one of the General Stores you find along Rte. 100 that most leaf-peepers become familiar with. She had recently told me it was her most prized possession. Best fifty dollars I ever spent.

The rise in her chest as she breathed reminded

me of the countless times of love making that ended with an arch of her back, eyes rolling, pursed lips holding back the ecstatic exhalation that, when released, sent her crashing back to earth with a glorious thud. The climax of two intertwined bodies powered by mutual lust.

A warm glow enveloped me as I thought about this, but my daydream was rudely interrupted by the tone from my phone indicating the arrival of a text message. I usually had alerts muted, but under the circumstances, I had to be available to friends and family.

The message simply said, "any change?" I thumbed back with, "status quo. she looks peaceful."

I checked to verify my assessment. I.V. lines were draped over the top sheet invading Pamela's arm and a morbid, corrugated breathing tube was sloppily taped to a mouth piece, hiding her supple lips. The different colored graphs that tracked her "signs of life" changed ever so slightly with each scan. Assuredly, not peaceful.

I added to my reply, "I'll let you know when..."

I took Pamela's hand. It was time to let her know again how I felt by telling one of the stories of our special bond. I closed my eyes.

"Babe, remember the time we went to the Zen Garden in Hubbardton last October? I thought it was a rumor and didn't exist. Seriously? A Japanese garden in some remote town in central Vermont only known as the site of a Revolutionary War battle? You had convinced me it was real and enticed me with the allure of a good hike to find out. You had insisted I include sushi, sake wine and chop sticks in my day pack.

I thought 'really', but you gave a Geisha-like

smile, fanned yourself and batted your eyes and cooed, 'Zen gardens can be very romantic.'

My knees buckled every time you got flirty with me."

It was a Vermont Postcard day. High puffy clouds bespeckled the deep blue sky only clean mountain air can produce. Foliage was peaking along with all five senses. The ochre blend of red, orange, yellow and colors-undefined carpeted the narrow trail. The bark of White Birches framed the magnificent autumn scene. It smelled like woods and streams and the coming snow. The trees echoed with a nearby brook succumbing to gravity over pebbles and boulders, neither offering the courtesy to get out of the way for fear the babble would go silent.

We crested a ridge and headed down. I explained to Pamela that the worst part about going down a tricky trail was you cannot enjoy the view above. I could, however, watch my wife effortlessly descend. Pamela was athletic yet graceful. The hiking boots, cargo shorts and a day pack she wore was the uniform of an angel meant only for me. She was a confident mountain lion leading her charge to a safe place.

"So lucky," I reminded myself aloud.

"What's that Babe?" Pamela looked back.

"I said, you're slow."

She tossed her head back and laughed as only she could then returned her attention to the terrain.

I paused, took a deep breath and gazed ruefully at my lovely mountain lion. Why? Why must you go? I have so many things I want to tell you. All I want are the things we have yet to do. I'm not ready to have only reminiscence as a partner and conversation as a monologue. My solace and pain is in knowing that we had something incomparable. As singular as a snowflake as extraordinary as the Northern Lights. I will never sort out how a lightning strike burst from the skies on our favorite golf course and snuffed your life like pinching a match with moist fingers. The flame was extinguished, yet emitting a wispy trail of smoke. An ember that cannot be rekindled.

I shook my head violently to expel these thoughts. I had all the imperfect time left on the clock to grieve. I brought myself back to our quest of a year ago:

The trail leveled out as the trees opened to a meadow. The field was bathed in sunshine and the lea grass was waving to us. We emerged and saw it. A garden. A Zen Garden.

I grabbed her hand. She used it to draw me in. We hugged and had a playful smooch. She pulled me closer and the little kiss became a deep and passionate probe of each other. What spell that made me transform from playful to wanton with a slight gesture was magic only Pamela had. We winked at each other acknowledging her earlier Japanese premonition.

The acre size garden was nestled on one side of a much larger field, bathed in the mid-morning sun. There were purposeful rocks with waterfalls, arched bridges over manicured streams and mini Pagoda's marking the center of flower beds. The valley was surrounded by the variety of Beech, Aspen, Red Oak and Maple trees. Nature's canvas painted with hues that made Vermont famous for such moments. There was no one else visible as if the proprietor's had hung the "Do Not Disturb Sign" on our discovery.

We sat on the bank of a Koi pond with lily pads perfectly staged. Dancing, black-mottled gold fish were blurred by the ripples made by our infringing toes. We ate sushi, drank sake and talked about all things Pamela & Me. We had been together for twelve years, yet there were still things we hadn't discovered about each other, or, more aptly, hadn't revealed to anyone before; the stuff of true love escalating; achievable by two ordinary people that are consummate as one.

An impish grin unfurled on Pamela that meant only one thing. We grabbed a fleece blanket and bounded off, giddy with lustful anticipation. We strode behind the boulder with a ribbon thin waterfall cascading into the Koi pool, then darted into the multi-colored tree curtain behind the rock, only a few paces into the woods. Before the blanket had been spread, our sweat soaked tee shirts and cargo shorts hit the leafy ground. Pamela's bare body still mesmerized me. Her milky-white skin was like the nearby Green Mountains in winter; a majestic panorama blanketed in fresh snow. A purely awesome sight that I would never tire of. Pamela's golden leaf necklace glinted as we immersed ourselves into each other. Our love had evolved to having passionate sex in semi-public places and become a favorite activity of ours. We had discovered this game together, so it felt as if it was ours alone. It was unbounded sensuality, daring and erotic.

The alert on my phone shattered my reminiscence. This time it was a calendar reminder. I looked at the perfect clock. It was too far away to be read. Time mattered more than any other time in my life. I referred to my phone. I had an hour. The Zen moment popped like an unsuspecting balloon falling on a bramble. My heart plummeted into a part of my stomach that wasn't there before. It was time to summon the family. I accessed the contact group I had prepared on my phone a month ago; the time we agreed as a family to not extend Pamela's suffering. I typed, "It's time" and hit send.

Soon after, the immediate family arrived. We gathered around the bed. I didn't have to think of anything to say because there was nothing to be said. We stood silently around Pam; a somber Halo made of family love encircling her.

Two nurses came in and touched my arm with a nod. I can't imagine anything like this ever becoming routine no matter how many times they have done this before. They disconnected the I.V. and the breathing tube along with all the other gizmos part and parcel of life support. Despite the instruments being muted, the silence grew tenfold. The rustling leaves became the soundtrack of saying goodbye. Pamela would have liked that I thought.

For the first time since the accident, I gazed at her face, unobstructed, save for my welling eyes. It took my breath away as she was about to be relieved of hers in a very different way. Freshly bathed, she had been dressed in a green "I Love VT" tee shirt, khaki cargo shorts and hiking boots. She was at peace and I would be too...some day.

I was told I had no more than five minutes. I checked the perfect clock to see if it offered more time. It didn't. I removed the gold maple leaf necklace from my pocket and put it around her neck. A fallen tear splashed on the gold surface. I brushed her hair back and kissed her forehead.

Good bye my love.

Saving Private Maloney

Mike Hotchkiss

Frank and Joe were face down in the muddy depression they had clawed out; the best version of a foxhole exploding shells and the persistent whiz of bullets would allow. The only other sounds were the variety of screams from soldiers being hit. The dissonance of armed conflict would be much worse except, thank God, men getting killed in battle made no noise.

Frank Pellegrini rehashed these thoughts in preparation for making his pitch for assistance to find his buddy, Joe. He arrived at the Allied camp at the foot of Monte Cassino, about 100 miles from Rome. There were soldiers from all over the place. Canucks, Poles, Indians, Aussies and Kiwis. No sign of Frank's 36th or any other Americans, but he knew some had to be here. He strained to search through a thick fog and cold drizzle that blanketed the camp as it had for the last four months in South Central Italy.

Frank walked around, saluting or tipping

his hat to all the foreign troops. He was the son of
Italian immigrants who had settled in Baton Rouge,
LA. He spoke Italian before English; whether an
omen or destiny of his current situation was unclear.

Frank spotted American olive drab uni's with
single and twin Chevrons on the shoulders. They
were circled around a fire attempting the impossible,
to stay warm and dry. He was scanned as he
approached the men. One Corporal noticed the blue
arrowhead with a "T" on Frank's shoulder. Likewise,
Frank noticed the blue crossed-eight shaped patch
on his counterparts' uniform. Division insignias had
become a badge of honor during the war. Blue meant
Infantry. In this war, blue insignias were highly
respected.

Frank decided to take the lead, "88th Infantry,
how do you do?"

"Hell 36th, we do just fine!" the Corporal
grinned in response.

"Frank Pellegrini." The 36th 'T-Patcher' introduced himself. "Glad you could make it from that
resort at Anzio beach," he mockingly added.

"Marty Obidinski, 'Obi'." Said the 88th Corporal. "Not as cushy as that river ride up the Rapido."

They both laughed and shook hands as the
other men around the fire closed in for slaps on the
soldiers. A rare time of hospitality to fellow soldiers
was welcome.

Frank got down to business and asked around
if they had heard about a Joe Maloney. With negative
head shakes, he pushed forward.

"Have you heard about prisoners? Word is
they are at a place called *Passo Carese*. Any of you
guys know about that?"

"That's a bad place," said Obi. "Lots of guys

go in and not a lot come out is what I hear. Why do you ask?"

Frank recounted his story about Joe Maloney, "I was badly wounded at the end of a two-day attempt to cross the Rapido River. Two-thirds of my Company, all friends of mine, were killed or wounded."

Frank and Joe had become best friends during three years of training from recruits at Fort Worth, TX in 1940 to a war against Nazi Germany in the failed Fascist state of Italy. Joe had saved his life on a few occasions and most certainly at the Rapido. Sharing every detail about Joe's past life and dreams ahead were etched in Frank's mind. He wasn't just trying to save his best friend, he was giving him a chance to live his dreams.

"The shell exploded outside our foxhole," said Frank. "I felt something hit my head and blood was streaming down my face. The head wound was minor, but the shrapnel that caught me in my belly wasn't. I woke up in the hospital and don't know what happened to Joe. The Army declared him *KIA*."

When he was done, Obi spoke, "Me and three of these guys are supposed to go on a recon mission towards Rome in the morning. If it's ok with the platoon leader, we can check out the prison camp; maybe find your buddy."

A short Lieutenant in the back nodded and in his native Oklahoman said, "The 88th ain't normally kind to y'all Texans, but ya got my ok to try to rescue yer friend. Just don't git my men kilt."

Frank had experienced help, the blessing of a superior officer and additional weapons.

~~~

The three soldiers from the 88th and Frank

were positioned outside Stalag 33 in Passo Carese about 25 miles north of Rome. They were wearing civilian clothes. US Army uniforms were far too recognizable behind enemy lines. They carried 1934 Barretta's courtesy of captured Fascist soldiers to complete the local farmer ruse.

Frank yielded operational authority to Obi. Corporal Jack, a crack shot from Tennessee, was armed with a Springfield M1903 Bolt Action sniper rifle. Known as "Volley", he would find the highest perch available within 500 yards – a comfortable kill range for him. "Sludge," a hand to hand combat specialist who knew German, would take the point. He would be with Frank and Obi at the breech point of the prison nearest the prisoner barracks. The fourth member, PFC Tico Hernandez was trained in explosives. He was dubbed "Taco" in basic training. He didn't have a specific assignment yet, but knew would be needed.

Sludge and Taco had just returned from a perimeter assessment around the camp. They had gotten close enough to overhear some of the guard's chatter.

Sludge reported, "It was mostly soldier talk, about being bored, not wanting to be here and having a particular dislike for the Commandant, "Spiegel" who was mentioned in the same sentence as chicken shit.

Taco added some grim news, "The Stalag is heavily guarded, both in patrols on the ground and watchmen in the towers. If there is good news, the buildings and fences are in a state disrepair."

Sludge continued, "We saw the guards march some of the prisoners out into the yard. This seemed to be a daily routine. They were marched around the yard with their hands shackled. They were gaunt and kept their heads down.

This last piece of intel was important because Obi had stressed that they will, at some time, need to rely on the strength and will of the prisoner to pull this off. This variable was in question.

"If Joe's in there, he'll know how to react," said Frank.

They made a plan. Risky, lacking proper resources and likely to end badly. No one complained.

Volley found a rock outcropping with a line of sight over the front gate and into the yard. He estimated he was over 700 yards away, but still felt in range. His perch set-up, he trained his M1903 towards the camp.

The other three men made their way to the back of the camp, about as far away from the gate as they could. The prisoners were kept in a row of barracks on the back side of the camp. There was no way to know where Joe Maloney was kept – if he was even there. The plan was for Frank, Obi and Sludge to work their way under the fence and sneak into the nearest barrack. They would need to do this silently. Taco was tasked with finding his way to the guard tower on the other side of the yard and set explosives. Radio silence meant Taco would have to use his judgment when and if to detonate. During the confusion, Volley would start picking off targets deemed most threatening.

The hoped-for result was to get as many prisoners out of the barracks and into the yard. Frank, Obi and Sludge would subdue as many guards as possible and hope to get the rest to drop weapons. If a full-blown firefight started, they were doomed.

The watches on all four men ticked to the top of the hour. The fence busters used their soldiers' spades to start digging. They had access in less than fifteen minutes. Taco was first under and set-off to the other side of the camp. The other three waited to be sure Taco wasn't spotted. He disappeared at the end of the row of barracks. It was time to go get the prisoners.

"ACHTUNG!" There were a series of clicks behind the men halfway under the fence. The distinct sound of German Gewehr 43's being set to fire. Frank looked back and saw at least eight kraut soldiers with weapons pointed at them. He backed from the tunnel with hands raised. Obi and Sludge followed suit.

Frank's brain kicked into overdrive. He figured the civilian clothes had probably saved them from being shot without warning. He pressed this thought and spoke in Italian, "Mi familia! My family is in there. We only mean to bring them food."

Frank didn't understand the response, but it was clear they were being asked to stand.

They were patted down and their guns confiscated. They did not find the hunting knife Sludge had inside his boot. There was no alarm from the Germans; either uncaring or undisciplined. Frank would get into the prison, but not in the way he had hoped.

Frank, Obi and Sludge were lead to the center of the yard and ordered to kneel. The Commandant of chicken shit fame emerged from a building underneath the guard tower. All eyes in the camp were trained on the three captives. Capturing locals poking around the fences was not an everyday occurrence. "Chicken-shit" and his Sidekick approached.

He spoke in a loud and harsh voice,
"You are enemies of the Third Reich! You are
spies. Who are you? Who ordered you here?"
This was translated into Italian by Sidekick.
Frank answered, "We are just farmers. My
brother and two sons were brought here as prison-
ers. We wanted to bring them food. We are no spies."
Sidekick translated. The Commandant
stepped forward and slapped Frank in the face.
"Nien! Spies. You are to be executed!"
He barked at the armed guards holding Frank,
Obi and Sludge at gunpoint. And then screamed at
the other soldiers who had appeared at the scene. A
dozen or more guards ran towards the barracks. The
emerged with a line of prisoners from each building.
There were to be witnesses to the execution.

It took some time to arrange the prisoners in
a semi-circle around the developing spectacle. Joe
Maloney was in the line of men led to the nearest
viewing point. He was looking at the men on their
knees before the commandant. They all appeared
resolved for something other than getting caught.
He thought, *those are no civilians.*

Frank gazed at the Commandant who had
pure evil in his eyes. He could tell the guards acted
out of fear to his orders, not respect. He turned to
survey the prisoners being organized around him
and immediately saw Joe. Their eyes met and they
nodded at each other indicating an understanding
of what was happening. Joe looked skinny, but his
pure green eyes still had the resolve of the fighter
Frank knew him to be.

Maloney leaned forward and looked up and
down the line of prisoners. He was slapped back into
place but not before he had established eye contact

with his fellow prisoners. Joe had taught them to save the single pat of butter along with bread the guards smuggled in once in a while. He demonstrated how the butter could be used as grease on their malnourished wrists to allow them to slide out of the shackles.

The Commandant barked some more orders. Guards in front of each group of prisoners recited a canned order in a variety of languages. Stalag 33 was multi-national too.

"By order of the Commandant Field Marshall Stueben Spiegel under the authority given by the Fuhrer, Adolf Hitler, these enemies of the state have been found guilty of treason and are sentenced to death by firing squad immediately."

Frank figured out their idea of a firing squad was a single guard with a Luger stuck in the back of his head. He looked at Joe who returned his gaze and winked. As he was figuring his friend's gesture, all the prisoner's shackles clanked to the ground. Frank took the cue as did Obi and Sludge, jumping from their kneeled positions and thrusting their heads into the gut of the armed men behind them. The line of prisoners leaped forward into the guards who were outnumbered by ten to one.

Spiegel raised his arm and yelled something, but was cut short. Frank glanced over and saw a red dot appear above Chickenshit's brow line. *'Nice shot Volley."*

An explosion went off under the guard tower. The tower along with guards came tumbling down. Chaos assumed control. Spiegel's Sidekick ran towards the struggle between Frank, Obi, Sludge and their executioners. He fell silently to the ground like a sandbag. *Volley again!*

Sludge had extracted his hunting knife and neutralized his executioner. He did the same to Obi and Frank's gunmen. They each grabbed a Gewehr 43 from the dead guards and shouldered the rifles; swinging around to find threats. The balance of the Germans in the company of the Commandant dropped their weapons and raised their arms.

Maloney and the other prisoners had gained control of most of their guards. The remaining ones seemed confused at first. They noticed what was happening in the center of the yard. Chicken Shit and Sidekick lay dead and their comrades were all dropping their weapons. They did likewise.

Suddenly the guards in the towers all lowered their weapons. Stalag 33 went silent.

The only thing audible was the sound of flames coming from the blown-up guard tower. Taco emerged from the smoke with a huge smile. Then, the front gates were opened by the unarmed German soldiers and Volley marched in with is M1903 over his shoulder.

Maloney took a brief survey of his fellow prisoners. Convinced everyone was ok, he walked forward to meet his friend. Joe and Frank met in the middle of the German Gulag in the Italian Countryside and shook hands. The remaining hands in the camp, including Joe's other rescuers from the 88th along with the Chickenshit hating guards, applauded.

Steps

Michael Hotchkiss

It was time to go. I'm not sure what prompted this. I was as popular as ice cream, I had lots of friends. I oozed confidence and possessed youthful energy more powerful than the sun. I took a step anyway.

It was a new place with lots of brick buildings connected by concrete paths that took me to social awareness. I met new friends; just as cool as the ones I had left. We were as smart as we were unwise. An interesting combination that yielded mostly joy. We celebrated nothing and everything. We played like careless fools. We shared secrets we didn't know we had. We fell in and out of love easily. Regrets did not exist nor did a cloud in the future. Time for another step.

I met serious people. Celebrations were fewer with more meaning. Love became more difficult yet more rewarding. Life had compartments. One with accolades, fancier clothes, and newer cars. This one motivated, rewarded materially. Another had life-purpose relationships; lasting, ones to savor, celebrated by milestones symbolized with cake or ceremony or newborns. Satisfying. Onto the next step.

I lost smarts and gained wisdom. Whims were less frequent and more calculated. I took many small steps at this stage. I found dragons on the water, a wall that could be seen from space, temples with beheaded statues, cities with rivers for streets. Obelisks, Mosques, a Leaning Tower, an Opera House in a picturesque harbor even a Forbidden City. I stepped into these places and met people, all intriguing, all with differing histories yet all rooted in the same Earth. I saw complexity, differences in appearances and experiences. Integrity coexisting with amorality. Compassion, anger, acts of kindness, abject hatred, squalor, opulence. I heard opinions, strange words with deep meanings, laughter that sounded the same in any language. I saw tears and years that flowed the same on different size and color faces. A universal diversity. Bizarre, amazing, baffling and satisfying. Flavors that stimulated like new discoveries. Exotic yet simple when viewed through the widest lens. A new step must follow.

I had gone back. It was dissimilar but the same. There were old friends and new acquaintances, but shallow were these. I left behind the better clothes and amazing experiences. I carried nothing from previous steps. Some intentional, some receding memories. Mediocre, untouchable, disinterested. Routine supplanted what remained of whimsy. A shell formed. I couldn't stop it. There were no celebrations. No accolades. No cakes or new life. New was no more. Smart and wisdom were dormant. I did not know despair until it grabbed me by the throat. Dark clouds were everywhere. I needed another step.

A gate unlocked and swung open and I walked out of the graveyard. The sun returned as did awareness. The interesting people were back. There to celebrate, share and laugh. Love became abundant. I was more wise than smart. I judged less and tolerated more. Inner calm over anger. The people of the past and present were alike: meaningful.

I took many steps and have many more to take.

I can't wait.

The Runaway

Michael Hotchkiss

Mimi awoke from an exhaustion induced slumber. Reality was creeping in amid the fog of a bad dream or a horrible memory; she wasn't sure which. She had spent the night in an alley using a partially full trash bag as a pillow and cardboard boxes as a mattress and blanket.

The rising sun created eerie shadows on the brick walls of the alley where Mimi had determined was the most suitable place to rest after roaming the streets of New Haven for the last 24 hours. Her consciousness rose with the lifting fog.

Mimi had run away from home. She was determined to find somewhere without rules or reprimands for reasons she did not understand. Rising clumsily from her cardboard mattress, she was reassured that she would find a better place, and soon. She gathered herself and set off.

Mimi was an orphan. She had spent the bulk of her young life at a facility called Hope House for orphans so was no stranger to tough living. The mission of Hope House was to find residents a foster home or adoptive parents.

She was kept in a small square space with four occupants matching the four corners where each would find refuge. If the room had eight corners, Mimi likely would have seven roommates. The conditions were cramped and turnover was high, so trust and relationships were not part of the growing process. She had food and water and the attendants tried to be as nice as a 16:1 caretaker to orphan ratio would allow. They were fed well and given play time outside. Fights would break out routinely, so Mimi kept her distance from the others. Trust would be a slow life skill to acquire.

Mimi had no recollection of any other living condition, so what was a bleak environment did not get the poor rating it deserved. She wasn't happy and she was lonely but didn't know it - never having felt differently. The best Hope House experience were visitors. Unbeknownst to Mimi, these were potential foster parents or even adopters. Introductions were made in a furnished "meeting room" with couches and tables. One corner had toys for the younger orphans to play with while they were being observed.

Mimi's personal attendant was named Sherry. Mimi liked her and wished she could have spent more time with her, but she had many others to look after. Sherry came and got Mimi one day and seemed very excited about something. They were heading to the meeting room.

When they entered, a young couple got up from the couch. Sherry beamed and approached the couple with her hand extended.

"Welcome to Hope House. I'm Sherry and you must be the Tharens – Phillip and Ophelia, right?"

"Why yes, we are. Please call us Phil and O"

Mimi was shy by nature and stayed near the door unsure of how to react. Sherry provided her cue, "Come here, Mimi. Meet your new friends."

Sensing Sherry's calm, Mimi walked over and stood next to Sherry leaning against her thigh for comfort. She looked up at Phil and O. It took less than a minute of smiles and praise for a match to be confirmed. Young orphaned Mimi was going to be a member of the Tharen family!

Phil and Ophelia lived in a rural section of New Haven. They both were professors at Yale University living in a comfortable Tudor style home. This gave them summers off; an ideal situation to acclimate their new family member.

Mimi was instantly overwhelmed. By her standards, the house was enormous. There was a large backyard to run and play. Ophelia showed her the house while talking to her the whole time. She gave Mimi reassuring touches saying "You're going to love it here little girl. We're going to do everything we can to make you as comfortable as possible."

After a few weeks, Mimi had mixed feelings. Her living conditions were far more comfortable and Phil and O had been exceedingly nice to her. However, she did not have anyone to play with. She even missed having roommates even though she had never paid much attention to those she lived with. She now had constant adult supervision. She was being taught so many rules. The easy life was a struggle. It's as if she had to always be happy and upbeat even after she was reprimanded for doing things that were never noticed at Hope House.

A few more weeks went by and Mimi couldn't shake the strange feeling of being watched all the time. She was supervised when she went out to play. She hasn't seen anyone her own age since she left Hope House. She was so accustomed to being on her own, this was becoming an adjustment she wasn't sure she wanted. She was suffocating.

Mimi was out in the yard playing. She hadn't noticed O slipping into the house returning with another lady. O called Mimi over and said, "Mimi, this is our neighbor Flo. She has a new adoptee too! Do you want to meet her?"

O took Mimi's indifference as a yes. Flo the neighbor disappeared through the back door and came back with her new charge in tow. She looked at Mimi and said, "This is Lucy; she's just about your age!"

Lucy gave Mimi a push prompting Mimi to scamper into the yard. Lucy continued shoving her until Mimi ran to the corner of the yard. Corners were safe, right? Unfazed, she chased after Mimi and pounced on her. Mimi let out a shriek. Lucy had raked her across the face. O and Flo took notice and realized this play date was not going as hoped.

"Lucy!" Flo yelled. "That is inappropriate behavior. Come here please."

Lucy trotted over to Flo with no sign of remorse.

"Sorry O," said Flo as she escorted Lucy through the door.

O replied "It's ok. It's a learning curve for all of us. We'll need to be more careful next time."

O stroked Mimi's hair and apologized profusely. It was clear she felt bad. She realized she was new at this Mom stuff and had made a mistake. Mimi became more anxious. Something had to change.

The change came soon enough. Ophelia was watching Mimi play in the yard through the kitchen window, when Phil had called out, "Dear O, come see this. I'm reading an interesting article on dealing with aggressive behavior of orphans. It might help getting Mimi and Lucy to play nice together."

O glanced out the window and reassured herself that Mimi was content outside so went to see what Phil was reading.

Not knowing or even carrying if O was looking, Mimi found her way to the back fence. The latch was disengaged and the gate opened with a gentle push. Mimi felt a wave of excitement. With no hesitation, she was out the gate and running as fast as she could. She felt liberated.

~~~

Optimistic again, Mimi left the alley and started on her quest to find a better place for her. As she wandered back onto the street, she tried to retrace her steps from yesterday.

She just knew she had gotten out of her yard and started running. She roamed for a long time. Grass yards and open streets were replaced with sidewalks and lots of noise. It smelled different. It was almost like not being outside anymore. She started to run past people. Some, if not most, called to her asking what was wrong or if she needed help. She ignored all the noise and kept moving. She soon learned that staying away from crowded streets and people was less intimidating.

Out on the street, it was the start of a work day and the sidewalk was packed with single-minded folks on their way to work. Surprised to go unnoticed, she was nonetheless frightened beyond any experience at Hope House or at the Tharens'.

Mimi needed to find space. She darted down another alley to get away from the throng. She heard sounds of people yelling at her. Stop! Wait! She was in full panic mode and started running again. She darted down another alley surprised to hear voices following behind her. She had to get away. She wanted to go back to where it wasn't scary. It was an instantaneous revelation. She wanted to get back to Phil and Ophelia.

The alley spilled into a large parking lot. With a glance behind her, Mimi saw she was being pursued by a handful of people all screaming for her to stop. It was like a bunch of Lucy's coming to jump on her. Look to the left, look to the right. Run straight ahead...right into the arms of a man in uniform. She squealed and squirmed but could not escape the iron grasp of the Policeman. The other pursuers had all caught up. They looked at each other asking, "Is she ok? What is she doing out roaming the in the streets?"

The officer asked them all to back away and give them space. Mimi continued to wiggle but not as forcefully. Her screams became sobs. A female cop showed up and started stroking the hair on her sweaty head and reassuring her she was going to be fine. The woman's touch worked as Mimi passed out from the emotions of fear and the physical exhaustion of running away.

~~~

It was now the morning after. Phil had returned once more from an all-night futile search. He had just gotten out of the shower when the doorbell rang. His hair still wet, Phil joined his sobbing wife in answering the door. Phil looked through the peephole and saw a police officer standing outside the door. Oddly, he was smiling.

They opened the door and saw a police car parked in front of the house. The officer asked, "Hello. Phil and Ophelia Tharen?"

O lurched in front of her husband and blurted, "Yes! Did you find our Mimi?"

"We sure did Ma'am!" he responded.

He looked over his shoulder at the cruiser and motioned his hand like a cop waving on traffic. The door opened and the female officer got out. The officer before them said, "You were very smart to have put a tag on Mimi with your address. You would be surprised how many dogs get lost without any ID."

Mimi jumped from the back of the police car and raced to the door with her tail wagging. She was home at last.

Carol Keeney

License to Drive 91

License to Drive

Carol Keeney

My father was happy that I was a late bloomer. At nineteen I was still not driving and that kept me safe. We lived in the Bronx and he saw that as his duty in life.

"Will you teach me how to drive? At least I can get a license someday."

He conceded to a learners permit and one lesson. One quiet Sunday he drove my mother, my brother and I to a quiet area around Lehman College. My mother and brother got out of the car, climbed a small hill and positioned themselves safely under a tree. My mother didn't drive and my father had learned at forty.

"OK Carol, come up and take the wheel. Let's see how you do."

My heart was racing but I tried to appear as calm as possible as I settled myself into the driver's seat of his small Buick sedan.

"Ok step on the gas and turn the key. The engine let out a loud roar. "No not like that! Turn it off and try again. This time barely step on the gas as you turn the key. The sound calmed down. "Now let me see you pull out and drive down the street."

My heart was in my throat but my determination to gain my freedom gave me courage. I turned the wheel and stepped carefully on the gas. We were moving! "Now turn it back so we're going straight down the street. You better listen to me Carol. You could kill someone if you don't know what you're doing."

My ears heard those words, but my mind blocked them. "You need to drive, or you'll never get out of the house."

As we drove down the abandoned street my Dad barked the next direction, "Now we're approaching a stop sign soon, make sure you stop. People fail the test automatically if they don't stop at a stop sign." I wasn't there but he began to repeat, "Stop, stop!" So, I did. I stopped right there.

"You're going to fail, Carol. You stopped too far from the corner. They'll fail you for that!"

"Forget it!" I snapped. "You told me to stop!"

"Ok, step on the brake and put the car into park." His voice was calm. The lesson was over.

I flung open the car door and jumped out. Turning back, I walked down the street and up the small hill to my mother. "He can't teach me." We went home. There would be no more lessons.

That summer I saved every penny from my summer job. One fall day I took a walk to a nearby driving school. I purchased a package of ten professional driving lessons. I let my mother in on my secret. She had always been too afraid to drive but I think part of her was rooting for me. Every time I left for a lesson she would beg me to be careful. When I returned home after the first lesson she was almost in tears "I heard the ambulances! Thank God you're home."

Mr. Rogers was like a yoga instructor. "Are you sure this is your first time driving? You seem like a natural."

"No, I've never driven but I always pay attention to other people's driving"

"Well you must have, because I would never know you hadn't been driving before!"

During my last lesson Mr. Rogers told me he had scheduled my driving test for the next week.

"Wow, what if I fail? I haven't even practiced. Would you give me one free lesson if I fail?" I laughed but I wasn't kidding. I had no opportunity to practice. I had to learn during those ten lessons.

"Don't worry, he assured me. You're a good driver and I'll put the driving school sign on the back that morning. They like that."

The memory of the test remains with me

today. "Parallel park right here." I pulled up close to a car and like a robot I turned the wheel and backed up. Then I turned it the opposite way and moving back, slid into the spot.

"Ok, move a little closer to the curb." This was a new challenge and I had not memorized the solution. I thought, "It's right or left, choose one." And just like that I chose wrong.

"Try the other way." I did. She continued, "That wasn't so bad, was it?"

I watched for the envelope from the Motor Vehicle Department to arrive for days and it finally did. I opened it up carefully. As I did I told myself I could buy another set of lessons next fall. But as I unfolded the official letter I saw the print was bold and black, "PASSED.

"I had won the lottery and held the winning notice as I walked into my apartment. I stood at the doorway of the living room and saw my father sitting in his brown reclining chair.

"Look what I got in the mail, a driver's license!" He didn't seem too surprised. He could do nothing to hold me back now. "OK, well now, all you need is to graduate and get a job, so you can buy a car. You're not borrowing mine."

Joseph Keeney

A Dead Christmas

Joe Keeney

Single in the mid-seventies, I was going out with a girl: Tracy was the kind of girl that went out with other guys and told you about it: to get your opinion. She invited me to her family's house for Christmas in Schenectady, New York. On one hand I was elated, and on the other hand I waited for the other shoe to drop, which it did: She confessed that she needed me to drive as her car needed repairs.

Tracey's dad was a big wig with GE which pretty much owned Schenectady. In addition, he owned a gas station and a funeral home there. We got there 11:30 pm to meet him outside an old house that looked like a funeral home.

Tracey's dad told me that they did not have room for me at his house because all the relatives visited for the Holidays. All they had on Christmas Eve to sleep in was an old funeral home, the one we parked in front of.

At 12 midnight with cold snowy wet feet, I trudged into the old house. Upon entry my nostrils were assaulted by a flowery mustiness smell. The kind that came from the visiter's flowers where the decease laid. Except for stupid me, there were no other visitors tonight: I hoped.

I followed dad to a second-floor room, it revealed metal gurneys on wheels pointing in all directions, the look of a clinic. I watched the snow fall out an open window as Tracey's dad covered one metal gurney with sheets and a pillow; I knew my time was short before I would be alone.

"No, I'll turn the lights out." I told her Dad firmly, as he left.

Alone, I went through the motions of stripping my pants and shirt off but my heart wasn't in it. The little pocket radio I brought -- I would be playing this sucker all night -- praying I'd forget where I was.

I laid awake on the gurney trying to pretend it was comfortable. Every rickety sound the old house made fought this delusion of comfort; instead, it made me wonder if there were other guests in the house, perhaps laying on gurneys in the basement.

At best, I slept a little before daylight, but who cares -- it was Christmas morning. I walked out of there in one piece.

-- God is good.

Moving Parts

Joe Keeney

The mall with hordes of Christmas shoppers would be the right place to do this. I could meld into the crowd and they wouldn't have a clue. Only I would know if it worked or not. As I pulled into the mall parking lot, I rehearsed one more time the words I would mentally repeat over and over once inside the mall: If you can read my mind, stop, stare at me and raise your left hand to your forehead.

In the food court I sat with coffee and newspaper in hand to avoid suspicion. Shoppers passed in a steady stream in front of me. And, just as steadily I focused on them, mentally saying: "If you can read my mind, stop, stare at me and raise your left hand to your forehead."

Nothing happened. NADA! Not even a stare back at me. A half an hour wasted.

I confess I felt silly.

But I was passionate because of what happened to me, courtesy of the US Army, years go. It was in a Florida hotel near Fort Lauderdale in the summertime.

But....I was not going to re-live it,not now.

Going down memory lane was superseded by the passion to find answers.

Maybe I would have better luck in another area of the mall. I found and sat at a little black table outside of a Starbucks.

Again, the steady stream of shoppers and I focusing on them repeated.

What? What just happened? A stare? Not exactly what I was looking for yet I thought I saw something.

Out of a group of shoppers, two men and a woman, the woman looked back at me as though she was confused; she raised her hand a little bit, too.

A waste of time, I thought. And, I decided not to waste any more of the afternoon on maybe's.

It happened to be in the food court where I started out, I found myself by the escalator that led to a mall exit.

About half way up the escalator, I told myself, "Oh hell, I'll just give it one more shot."

"If you can read my mind, stop, stare at me and raise your left hand to your forehead."

A woman who appeared to be 21 years old, at that precise moment, was eyelevel with me as she descended the escalator on the other side. She turned her head and stared at me, she looked straight into my eyes and raised her left hand to her forehead.

Something bolted through me like a shot of adrenalin. I got red in the face as though my blood pressure sky-rocketed. I forced my neck back, to get a look at her, but it was no good. she turned her head straight and descended to the food court and got off the escalator. I never saw her again.

On my drive home, I was high on the idea that I transmitted thought, and I couldn't wait to try it elsewhere. And, I wanted to know if it worked the other way – me as receiver, too.

As I distanced myself from those Christmas shoppers and the mall, one idea brought me down real fast with trepidation.

Christmas shoppers don't dress like the young woman on the escalator did. They don't wear army fatigues!!!

Debbie Tosun Kilday

A Time Forgotten 105

A Time Forgotten

Debbie Tosun Kilday

It was the coldest winter that we had ever experienced in our 40 some years of living in the Northeast. Maybe in reality it was not as cold, but this year we were noticing it. John had been laid off for four months, and me for the last eight months. We did not know where to turn for help. People usually give to different charities, but not to people they know. This is what we had found out. We had both asked family and friends for help, but instead of help, we got comments like, "Why didn't you think ahead to the future" or "My motto has always been to live within your means". All we were getting was advice, but advice doesn't put food on the table or keep you warm. We needed real help, and there was none to be found. Soon we would leave our beloved home due to the bank foreclosing on us. It was home to my Great-Grandmother and Great-Grandfather who had passed on long ago. I barely remembered them now except through photos, but now we had other things on our minds besides reminiscing over photos. Our youngest son was to arrive home for the holiday weekend with two friends from college. We had nowhere to send our son off to, and were ashamed to tell him there was no heat and no food in the house. Both John and I had slipped into a depression trying not to face what had become of our lives. The alternative would have been to just give up and give in. We were fighters even though we were fighting a losing battle it seemed.

The next morning our son Josh arrived, bag of laundry slung over his shoulder for Mom to do. I had forgotten to tell him that the washer and dryer had been broken for the last several months. Both John and I were so happy to see Josh we hugged and kissed him as if it was the last time we would. Josh said, "It is freezing in here. Someone turn up the heat". Then Josh introduced us to his two college friends, Barry and Luke. Barry was from England and Luke from Scotland. That was the reason they could not easily go home for the holiday weekend. I told Josh that he and his friends would be staying downstairs in his old room in the basement. I knew I would have to explain our situation to Josh, but John and I were dreading it. Josh seemed to be happy despite the cold house he came home to. The three boys bounced down the stairs talking and laughing. It was good to hear laughter again. Almost as soon as Josh had bounced downstairs, he was running upstairs all out of breath.

He exclaimed, "Since when did you rent out the other half of the house to those two old people? Don't get me wrong Mom and Dad, I know things have been a little tough for you guys, but who are those people?" John and I didn't know what to say. We had not rented out any part of our house to anyone. We all rushed down the stairs and then up the other set of stairs going to the third floor attic of our house that had been closed off to try and save the heat from escaping. As we arrived, the first thing we noticed was it was warm, and the old fireplace that had been abandoned, was now lit and burning. My great-Grandmother's old dining table was set up with her handmade tablecloth she had crocheted, and candles were lit and burning. Before I could say anything or even think, two elderly people came into the room. No one had to tell me their names. Sarah with her reddish hair swept up into a bun, her stockings rolled down to her knees, was wearing a white cotton apron. James with his gray hair, glasses on his nose, was holding his unlit pipe. Had we frozen and passed on, I asked myself? Maybe so, but everyone else was seeing the same thing at the same time. The two elderly people were my great-grandparents that had passed on long, ago. Instead of my heart stopping, I took a deep breath. I said to Josh and John, "This is Sarah and James. They have been staying here for a long time but I barely see them, so I didn't mention it". Sarah said, "I need you boys to help get some chairs to put around this table before dinner is ready." The three boys including my husband John, all rushed to offer any help that was needed. James said, "I am getting up there in age, so I can't do it myself any longer." Sarah turned to me and said, "Would you be a dear and go get the good china, the pink with the roses on it, out in the china closet and my silverware out of the buffet and set the table?" Then she added, "Don't forget the linen napkins. This is a special occasion." I decided I would not disclose the identity of our newly-found roommates. It was warm, food was cooking, and everyone was happy, so why should I spoil it? Everyone chipped in to help Sarah and James and everyone was comfortable. When dinner was ready I helped Sarah make the gravy for the turkey with the drippings that were left in the pan. If this was a dream, I was not waking up at the moment. Josh said to Sarah and James, "Don't you guys have a TV? What do you do for fun?" James said, "We do the old fashioned thing called having a conversation." Everyone laughed. While sitting at the table and eating dinner, Sarah and James told the boys of the time of the Great Depression. Their lesson was, no one would have survived it, if people had turned their backs on others. They took them under their wing helping those in need with what little they had to offer. Sarah said, "We didn't have a lot, but what little we did have, we all shared." I wished that were true in today's world, but people have seemed to have forgotten about their family, friends and neighbors altogether. Instead of embracing people in need they abandon them never to look back. After dinner we all sat around the warm fire as James read stories aloud from an old book. I helped Sarah wash the dishes and John dried them. Josh and his friends put them away under Sarah's direction.

Sarah and James told everyone to get a good night's rest and be up early to have breakfast with them. Sarah took several of her handmade quilts and handed them out to us as we were going downstairs to bed and said, "Don't forget to bundle up, it's cold".

The next morning we all got up to the smell of bacon frying. Eagerly we all rushed upstairs to see Sarah and James, and spend time with them. Everyone chipped in with the chores. Josh was surprised to find that his clothes had been washed and were hung in the rafters, drying. Josh said to me, "Mom, Sarah and James are the coolest old people I ever met even though they took and did my laundry." My reply was, "Just go with the flow, I am."

The weekend went by in a flash and Josh and his friends were headed back to college. After saying our goodbyes, Josh and his friends were packed up and gone. Standing in our doorway waving our good-byes to Josh as he and his friends drove off, John turned to me and said, "Why didn't you tell me about Sarah and James?"

I replied, "I had forgotten all about them to tell you the truth." John looked at me puzzled. We both went into the house and started cleaning up after our weekend visit with Josh and his friends. John said, "We better get these quilts back up to Sarah and James. I appreciate everything they did for us this weekend." I turned to John and said, "Wait, I want to go with you." As we walked up the stairs, it was quiet. When we got to the top of the stairs, John was about to knock, but I just turned the doorknob to go inside. John was shocked, but I was not. Everything was as it was before Josh's visit. Everything was packed up and untouched. The fire was out and it was cold up there.

John turned to me and said, "Where did they go?" I said, "I want to tell you an unbelievable story." He said, "I'm listening."

I started telling John about Sarah and James and went to get the old photo album to show him their pictures. John exclaimed, "How is it possible?" I replied, "I am not really sure, but they were here when we needed them most, I guess."

Weeks went by with no signs of Sarah and James

as both John and I checked the upstairs apartment once a day. The New Year was upon us and the temperature was rising just a bit. John and I had just come back from the bank trying to get them to consolidate our loans into a more affordable one. As we approached our home we saw our neighbors coming out of our house. John turned to me and said, "I'll call the police." "Let's see what is going on first", I said.

The middle-age couple that lived in the beige house up the hill were talking to each other and seemed to be waiting for us to approach. "Hi neighbors", exclaimed the couple. The man said, "Hi. I'm Dan, and this is my wife Jody." Then the woman said, "I'm sorry we haven't been friendlier all these years. I guess we all were wrapped up in our own lives. Your boarders, Sarah and James told us not to use the back entrance and instead go down the stairs through your house. I hope you don't mind?" John replied, "Not at all, not at all." I asked, "How do you two know Sarah and James?" They both replied in unison, "Sarah has been teaching our granddaughter who has been visiting, how to crochet, and Dan gets some good advice on woodworking from James." "Oh good", I said.

Even though the subject of Sarah and James seemed to be the icebreaker, both John and I found ourselves talking with our neighbors telling them about our situation.

Jody said, "Dan works at the bank downtown. Maybe he can get someone to take another look at your loan."

After our conversation with the neighbors we ran into the house down the stairs, up the other flight of stairs and turned the doorknob. Sarah and

James were standing there waiting for us in their apartment. After embracing them both Sarah said, "You two just needed some help, so we are here, but you will be alright now." James nodded in agreement.

Sarah took me by my two hands and sat me down telling me how she was planning a going away party for her and James and how the whole neighborhood would be invited. John and I just listened.

The party for Sarah and James arrived a few weeks later. People John and I had never seen or met were arriving at our house. Neighbors carried in food on trays, and everyone seemed to have a story of what lesson they had learned from Sarah and James and how they would miss them. John was offered a job by Dan, and I was hired as a secretary a few weeks later. We never forgot the lessons we learned from Sarah and James. It reminds us of a time forgotten, when people cared as much about each other as they did about themselves.

Neal McCarthy

Winter Springs 115

Winter Springs

Neil McCarthy

Melissa looks up from her Sunday morning paper and her warm cup of coffee to gaze out the window at the family orchard. "It's not supposed to be this warm, Harold," she worries aloud to her husband sitting across the breakfast table.

"Oh, let's just enjoy it while it's here," he says quietly. "The boys are having a nice time playing out by the trees. So the weather's a little warm for February. We need to be okay with that. We both knew this was coming someday."

"But... the apples... Jamie... Ian. What if they don't grow this year?"

"Oh, Melissa, hun. You're overthinking this. Everything is going to be fine. Can you please hand me the front section?" Harold opens the paper and reads. "Hmmm... Says it's going to be warm most of the week. That is something. Well, I guess we'll have to do what we always do.

"What's that?"

"The best we can."

"I suppose you're right. You off to your winter job now?"

"Yup, I'll be in my office if you need me."

"You still developing websites?"

"Uh-huh."

"How much time does that take anyway, to bring in some extra money?"

"I suppose it takes the amount of time needed for the job to be complete, just like anything that bears fruit," Harold smiles. "Let me know if you need any help with the boys."

"Oh, I think they're old enough now that they don't need so much attention, but I'll give you a holler if anything comes up." Melissa brushes some brown hair from her face and gets up to take a shower.

Harold walks past the bathroom down the long hall to his office. He ducks his head to clear the short doorway, his last remnants of black hair on the back of his head angling away from the floor.

He sits behind his modest desk, turns on the computer, and begins to... do nothing. Melissa does not know he mostly does nothing back here, but Harold had discovered that if he sat alertly and attentively, then he would be ready for anything that comes. His thoughts slow dramatically as he focuses on his breathing. He sits like this for almost two hours, smiling, until an email pops up asking him to complete a task. He works at a rapid, efficient pace, completing the task in short time. I'll send that back later. They'd probably give me a lot more work if they knew I was finishing this so quickly.

The family of four gathers for lunch. The older one, Ian, speaks up first. "It's pretty warm out there, Dad. Do you think the trees will bud early this year?"

"Not sure, sport. What do you think, Jamie?"

"Could happen," says the younger one between bites of peanut butter and jelly on white bread.

"Ian, Harold," says Melissa. "Let's talk about nice things at lunch."

"Right you are, my dear. So, what were you kids going to do with the afternoon?"

"Wiffle ball!!" they answer excitedly together.

"Sound good to me. Please clear your plates when you're done eating."

Ian looks up from his sandwich. "Sure thing, Dad."

Jamie sighs exasperatedly. "Fine, Dad."

Three days of warm weather bring concern to the Sumner family—at least the mother and two sons. With no evidence of frost, the trees seem ready for a late winter budding. Harold walks slowly between the neat rows of trees, each decorated with its own color ribbon denoting the type of apple it yields. He looks down and shakes his head, briefly caught up in what could be the consequences of the day.

Then he remembers that maybe, all is well, and that all is as it should be. He smiles and turns off the mental chatter, walking deliberately. One step, breathing in. Yes. Two steps, breathing in. Yes. One step, breathing out. Thank you. Two steps, breathing out. Thank you.

Melissa looks out the window as he walks away. She looks at the warm ground, shakes her head, and stares sullenly at the sink. What IS he doing out there? And how is this helping? Isn't there something we can do to keep the trees from budding?

Day five of the warm winter spell brings apparent catastrophe. On a Thursday morning, the family of four stands in their orchard and sees buds! Not all the trees are showing signs of early growth, but many do.

"What are we going to do?!" A distraught Melissa asks.

"I don't think there's anything we can do." Replies her less concerned husband. "If the trees want to bud, we must let them."

"But this must not be the only place where trees are budding... In winter! Who knows what else might be growing out there now?!"

"No one does. Look, I understand you're upset, dear, but we must let it be. We need to keep calm about this so that our next decisions will be the most appropriate ones."

"But what about money, Harold? How are we going to pay the mortgage?"

"Mom?" interrupts Jamie, the eight year old. "Are we going to starve?"

The mother rubs her son's back gently. "I don't really know at this point, my love. We're going to have to wait and see. This is a larger, more global problem. Trees weren't meant to bud in the winter."

Ian, the ten-year-old frowns. "What are we going to sell in the market? Are we going to open it early?"

His father keeps his cool. "That's a possibility, Ian." He smiles. "Maybe we'll open up everything early. Great idea! Let's wait and see what happens and roll with it."

"Wait and see?! Wait and see?!" Melissa interjects. "We need to do something, and fast!

"Well, this is February. I'm not sure there are

enough hours of sunlight to grow anything substantially right now, even if the ground did stay warm. Let me go do a little research on the computer to see how much daylight is needed. I'll be in my office."

Harold breathes deeply and returns to his place of solitude. He sits comfortably in his upright office chair and relaxes his body. Taking in a full breath, he smiles again. He feels his breath all the way down in his toes, and as he inhales, he brings the sensation up through his body to the top of his head. With the exhalation, he sends the feeling back down to his toes. He calms his entire being as if it were a piston, moving up and down, breathing in and out. Smiling, Harold's mind slows to imperceptible activity, along with his ego. The only thought that arises is Who am I? His shoulders drop and his jaw hangs open.

On the sixth day, the once unimaginable happens. A cold front comes in, and, with the family unable to protect all the trees, frost sets in, killing perhaps the entire year's bounty. "Now what?" asks Melissa as the four stand by the window.

Harold gives her a long embrace and kisses her on the head. "I don't really know, sweet. It doesn't looks like we will have many apples for this year, so we'll have to figure out something else to do."

Two children and a mother hang their head in sadness. Unbeknownst to them, the father looks out at the orchard and smiles again. "Listen, family, everything is going to be okay. Things will be fine. Things are fine. Being dejected is only going to complicate matters. We need to keep our heads about us and simply come up with another plan."

Melissa dots her eyes with a tissue. "Harold, you're a sweet man. But I just don't see how we, or many people, can survive in these conditions. I mean, if there is no fruit here, then maybe lots of food might be struggling to grow in many places."

"You make some good points, my dear, but if there is no life right here in this present form, then it simply moves somewhere else. Maybe we find another way to live, or maybe we go somewhere else. But we need to have faith that everything will work out. My recent experiences tell me that they undoubtedly are already. I know it might be hard for you to see that right now, but we mustn't be blinded by only looking at what is right in front of us. There is so much to life that we are not aware of. If we open ourselves up to the possibilities of the universe, then we may see that there is no need to worry."

"Dad?"

"Yes, Jamie."

"How do we see what is not there?"

"We find another way of looking. There is more space in the universe than there is matter, so we could start looking there and simply experience the wonder of what might be. Now if you'll excuse me, I'm going to my study. Maybe there is a another job I can find through the computer."

Saturday morning finds the family eating breakfast quietly together. The two boys look glumly down at their bowls, unable to eat their cereal. Their mother, also with no appetite, stares out the window, lost in thought.

Harold, however, eats his granola, smiling and savoring every bite, not sharing his family's grim outlook. "Say boys, it's Saturday. How about we play a little wiffle ball?" No one answers. "Basketball, maybe? There's still that old hoop above the barn... No?"

Melissa is beside herself. "How can you be so chipper?! Not only could we lose everything, lots of people could starve, too."

Harold scratches his scruffy chin. "Hmmm... I understand your frustration. But, would you somehow feel happier if I were in a sour mood?"

"Well, no, hun, but... Look around you. All the trees could be barren this year. This is no time to be playing games."

"Oh, but it is, my love. It is always time to have fun. If we weren't having fun with our lives, then, what would we be having? Stress? I say; there is no time for that. I say, we must live our lives to the fullest, and not lament if, or when, we might move on to next one. Look outside right now, and, each of you, and tell me what's not wrong today."

Ian glances outside. "Well, Dad. The sun's shining."

Jamie adds, "And there's birds at the bird feeders."

Harold looks intently at his wife, waiting. Finally, she speaks. "There's no snow."

"That's the spirit, everyone. Now, what if I was to tell you that there is a way out of this mess, that there is always room for joy?"

"That'd be pretty great, Dad," says Ian. "Are we going to get our apples back?"

"Not sure if we can do that, son. But I can show you something better."

"Stop teasing us, Harold. What is it?" asks Melissa.

"Okay. Let's just say I've been getting a lot of

on-the-job training lately, and there are a few tricks I've picked up that might be of use to everyone here. Would you like to learn them?"

"You mean about web development, Dad?" asks Jamie.

"A little bit of that, maybe, but something even better. You see, I can show you where all the secrets to your life lie if you know where to look." No one answers.

"Okay then, you can either stay here and be depressed, or I can show you why I'm the only one here who isn't. How about that?" The boys and his wife nod, gaining interest.

Harold finishes the last of his granola, and, smiling, stands up from the table. "Alright family, there's nothing we can do out there about this, so let's see what we can find when we go in here." He takes his wife by her hand and leads the whole family to his office to cultivate in them the awareness he has been experiencing over that past few years.

Beverly Peck

Insomnia

Beverly Peck

I am in Somnia
an insomniac in Somnia
a place where sleep comes knocking
on a door that's sealed shut.
Where creepy, crawly thoughts abound
dull aches and pains assail around
a soul that's tethered to the ground
that's gritty with defeat.

Clocks chime in Somnia.
People cry in Somnia.
If someone dies in Somnia
do they rest in peace?

Confronting in Somnia
rising up in Somnia
counting sheep in Somnia
one million armored sheep.

Breaking free in Somnia
shattering in Somnia
falling, falling
free falling
falling
fast
asleep.

Rebellion

Beverly Peck

In the beginning
it would have been too much
to ask the colors to stay
quiet and subdued in the heavens.

It would have been unjust
to ask red, yellow, and purple
to wait patiently to be called earthbound.

It would have been a crime
to keep orange, green, and indigo blue
away from human touch.

And so, one mercifully lucid moment
in a darkness like night
in a timeless time
the colors of San Miguel de Allende conspired.

They pleaded their cause
vowing to bring honor to their Creator
and beauty to what might lack it.

They vowed to make a difference
even as they banded together
trembling.

In a Word, it was done
a bloodless coup.

The colors descended
some boldly alone
others, white with fear, running together.

Thankfully, the colors kept their promise.

The sun rose smiling
to a San Miguel morning
where nothing ever appeared the same again
where endless possibilities for creativity continue to
abound.

Bill Rockwell

Fetch 131

Fetch

Bill Rockwell

The voracious beach sand slurped when it swallowed Jeremy whole and live.

The day had started with violence and darkness as a summer thunderstorm roared into existence. The weathermen, who had predicted a beautiful day with the highs in the 80's, had no explanation for the rash weather, or its sudden disappearance only fifteen minutes after beginning. They immediately informed the vacationers along the shoreline of Connecticut to enjoy the day since no further weather disturbances were expected. Despite this reassurance, an ominous black cloud hung over the beaches.

As he walked along the shore of Osprey Beach, Darren dragged his toes through the warm, white sand, leaving deep furrows in his wake. His eyes scanned the wet sand for any jellyfish, or broken shells. Don't want to step on any of those...too painful.

Birdie, a three-year old Black Lab, pranced

around him, wagging his tail, and repeatedly jumping against Darren.

"What is it, Boy? Do you want to play fetch?"

Birdie jumped excitedly. Darren searched for something to toss. Spotting a foot-long stick floating along the shore, Darren pointed.

"There, Birdie. Fetch. Go get the stick, Boy."

Birdie bounded into the surf, grabbed the stick mid-jump, and swam back to shore.

"Bring the stick here, Birdie. Come! Bring it to me."

Birdie dropped the stick at Darren's feet. Birdie then backed off in leaps and bounds, awaiting Darren's lob. Darren hurled the stick well into the pounding surf. Birdie didn't hesitate. He started his run as soon as he detected the direction of Darren's toss, his gaze fixed on the stick. He dove into the water, bounding twice before being forced to swim. Grabbing the stick between his giant teeth, he reversed direction, made for shore, and sprinted back to Darren.

They repeated this exercise several times as they proceeded along the shoreline until Birdie abandoned the stick to investigate a large Conch shell, lying on the dry sand. He sniffed it once, and began a low, guttural growl as he held his haunches high, and placed his chin close to the sand.

"What'd you find, Boy?"

Darren ran to Birdie's side, slowing his approach when he heard the tone of Birdie's growl.

Birdie never growls. What gives? "Pretty shell, huh, Birdie?"

Darren reached for the pure white shell. It shone brilliantly, as if under the noonday sun instead of the dark sunless sky presently overhead.

The shell suddenly changed color, first to iridescent pink, and then blood red, some of the crimson liquid dripping onto the sand. Birdie barked so loud that it hurt Darren's ears. He then grabbed Darren's wrist, biting harder than he had intended, and pulled him away from the Conch.

Darren pushed Birdie with his other hand. "Hey. Let go of me. You don't bite me...ever."

Birdie released the arm, but continued growling at the shell. Darren rubbed his wrist. Birdie had left teeth marks, but hadn't broken the skin.

"What's wrong? It's only a shell, and a pretty one at that. I've never seen one change colors, though." He glanced at Birdie. "Did you know that if you hold a shell up to your ear, you can hear the ocean?"

Birdie responded with two loud, sharp barks, placed his tail between his legs, and ran down the beach, turning after a few yards to see if Darren had followed. He hadn't. Birdie hurried back to him, and tried to grab his wrist again. Darren yanked his hands high into the sky, and danced in circles as Birdie leapt against him. He caught Darren's shirt on one jump, and began tugging on it.

"Hey. Stop that. Don't rip my shirt; it's one of my favorites. Leave me alone. What's the matter with you anyway?"

A sudden, high-pitched voice sprang from the shell. Both froze. Darren grabbed Birdie's collar, and pried his shirt from Birdie's teeth. The shirt remained undamaged.

"Did you hear that, Birdie? Is that what you're trying to tell me, that there's something in the shell? I've never heard the ocean without putting it to my ear before. Maybe this shell is special."

He pushed Birdie away, but the dog returned, never taking his gaze from the shell, or his loud growl. Darren repeated his push, and while Birdie tried to regain his footing, he grabbed the shell. It vibrated in his hands, and returned the to its deep red color. He could feel no moisture, only slick shell. Birdie sat before him, his growl low, but noticeable. As Darren raised the Conch to his ear, Birdie stretched out on the sand, his chin again lying on his front legs, his eyes glued to the shell.

Darren expected the sound of waves crashing against rocks. Instead, a child's voice resonated from deep within the shell. "Help. Help me."

"Jeremy? Are you in there?"

He had left his younger brother back at the rental cottage, or had he?

"Is that you Jeremy? Is there a cell phone in there? Could this shell be some new kind of phone?"

He inspected the Conch by running his hand over its spiral curves. He could find no charging cord, or earphone jack. As a matter of fact, he found no metal of any kind. He looked deep into the shell. Nothing.

"Help. Darren, help me."

"Where are you, Jeremy? I don't see you. Is this some kind of joke?"

He looked back toward their cottage. He saw no one.

"Help. Help me."

Suddenly, the Conch began to bleed again, the blood flowing from its tip, pouring a huge amount of the liquid onto the sand. Darren tried to drop the shell, but it stuck to his hands as if glued. He shook it. Nothing.

"Let go of me."

Birdie leapt to his feet, barking ferociously. He jumped, striking the shell and Darren's hand simultaneously with his snout. The Conch dislodged, falling to the beach with a quiet 'thud.' Darren fell on his back with Birdie on top of him.

Darren checked his hand for any sign of the red liquid. None. Suddenly, the sand around the shell began to swirl, forming a fast-moving whirlpool. It's border expanded quickly. Darren sat up, and tried to crawl backwards away from the whirlpool's edge. Birdie grabbed the back of his collar and pulled. The whirlpool, however, grew faster than their retreat, soon encompassing Darren's legs, hips, and then his body. As he began slipping into the crevice, he groped the sand around him, hoping to find something solid to grab, something to use for leverage against the pull of the whirlpool, anything to keep him from being eaten by this hungry beach. He found none, his hand filled each time with fine sand. He reached above him, grabbing Birdie's collar.

"Pull, Birdie. Pull."

Birdie pulled harder, but also couldn't get anything firm beneath his paws. As the sand sucked Darren over the edge, Birdie refused to release his shirt. The collar finally tore, severing their connection.

"Ahhh. Help!"

Birdie jumped headfirst into the whirlpool after Darren. Both fell, somersaulting downward into the pit, accompanied by bloodstained sand that bombarded their faces, filled their mouths, and effectively silenced them. Both closed their eyes against the sandstorm, and lost track of the other.

After a few minutes, Darren landed in soft

sand face down, sinking almost a foot before stopping. He pushed himself up so he could peer above the red sand.

"Birdie? Birdie, can you hear me?"

Nothing.

Darren scrambled to his knees. Nothing hurt. He looked up to discover total blackness in the ceiling high overhead. He could see no evidence of the whirlpool, or a passageway to the beach. The red, luminescent sand provided the only light. He inspected his hands. No red stains. He found the same with his now tattered-at-the-neck shirt. He stood, carefully at first to ensure he wouldn't sink farther into the soft sand. He didn't. One seemingly endless passageway led away. A stale smell filled his nostrils.

"Birdie?" No response. He yelled louder. "Birdie?"

He listened for any reply. None. He took a cautious step, finding the sand hard packed. He ran his hand lightly against the wall, afraid of dislodging any loose sand that would lead to a collapse that might bury him. It felt warm, but solid. No sand dislodged no matter how hard he rubbed.

"Where the heck am I?" He yelled down the corridor. "Birdie? Jeremy?"

He heard a faint crackling in the distance. He listened carefully.

"Help."

"Jeremy, is that you?" No response. "I'm coming."

He started walking, looking back occasionally until he could no longer see the point of his impact. He broke into a trot, then a full sprint.

"Coming, Jeremy. Birdie, can you hear me?"

Nothing.

The corridor turned, and ended at a junction with five others, all seemed to be lit with the same red sand. The ceiling rose far above him.

He froze, muttering to himself, "Which way?"

"Help."

The voice had come from the passage on his right. He followed the voice as it directed him to a side shaft, then another branching corridor, and then another. He lost track of how many turns he had finally made, much less in which direction they had occurred. He finally spotted a red clearing ahead, and slowed.

"Help."

"Is that you, Jeremy?"

He proceeded into the clearing to find Jeremy standing in its exact center. He ran toward him. Jeremy held up his hand to stop him. It didn't work. Darren ran into an invisible barrier, bouncing back onto the ground. He rubbed his nose.

"What happened?"

"I can't get out. It's some kind of force field like in the space movies."

"How'd you get in there? Who put you there, and why? And how do we get you out of here?"

Jeremy began crying. "I don't know who, or why. All I know is I found a shell outside our cottage this morning, and the sand swallowed me. This is where I fell." He bawled louder. "I don't know how to get out. Mom's going to kill me for going onto the beach alone."

"Stop crying. You're ten years old, too old for crying."

"Yeah, like you never cry. I've seen you cry, and you're twelve. So, I can cry if I want."

"Yeah, I suppose so, but that's not going to help us get out of here."

A deep, resonant voice echoed behind Darren. "No, but I know someone who can help you with that."

Darren spun. Jeremy backed away until he hit the rear of his invisible chamber.

Darren shook with fear. "Wh…Who are you?"

The man, dressed in a white uniform covered with short, curved, black streaks, stepped toward Darren. He carried a wand in one hand. He extended his hands as he stopped several feet in front of the children.

"I'm Professor Quinta, better known to the world as Wizard Quinta. I presume you've heard of me?"

Darren shook his head. Jeremy remained frozen with fear.

"Oh, how unfortunate….for you, that is. I'm known as a world class Wizard. I brought both of you here using my wizard powers." He raised the wand over his head. "A simple wave of my wand, a few magic words and, presto, you're here."

Darren examined the wizard through suspicious, beady eyes. "That's not what happened to me. I fell after I found a Conch shell. I didn't hear any magic words, or see you there."

Quinta began a slow circuit of the room, as if lecturing to an appreciative audience. "That's because I couldn't be there to extend my invitation to you."

Darren kept a watchful eye on Quinta. "Invitation? What invitation?"

Quinta stopped, and spread his arms. "Why, the Conch shell's invitation, of course."

Darren took a cautious step toward the wizard. "Here. Where is here anyway?"

"It's...simply...here. I thought you'd like a visit, that's all."

Jeremy ran to the front of his cage. "I'd like to go home now. That's what I'd like."

"Yeah, me too. Wave that wand of yours, and send us back to the beach. Our parents are going to be mad. They're probably searching for us right now. My dad is strong. He can beat up any wizard, any day."

"I'm sure he can, but he won't get the chance." He placed both hands on his hips. "Your family is what I wanted to speak to you about, your father in particular, and, more importantly, you, Darren."

"Dad? Me? Why didn't you simply come over for dinner? My mom makes great, homemade pizza. You didn't have to kidnap us."

"Kidnap? Is that what you think I did. No, no! I sent an invitation you couldn't resist via my Conch shell. By the way, did you like it?"

"Which part, the part where it bled all over me, or sucked me down here to...to...wherever this place is? No, I didn't like it, and if you think waving a wand around like Merlin, The Magician, impresses me, it doesn't. Wizards are only in the movies and TV. Anyway, if you were a real wizard, you'd have simply brought us here directly, or showed up in our cottage, not tricked us into this sand trap."

"Not impressed, huh? That's too bad. Oh, well, maybe you'll understand after I explain."

Darren took another brazen step forward. "We don't want to understand. We want to go home, now!"

The wizard strode toward Darren, his frown

deep and threatening. Darren retreated until he abutted Jeremy's invisible chamber.

"Now you listen to me, You Twerp. I invited you here to listen, and you're going to listen, and do what I say, or you're going to be trapped down here like I've been for hundreds of years."

Darren turned toward Jeremy. He twirled his forefinger around his temple, mouthing 'crazy' to him.

"We're not staying. Let Jeremy out, or I'll call my parents on my cell phone."

The wizard laughed. "Go ahead. There's no service down here anyway."

Darren tried, but only confirmed the lack of signal. As he placed the cell phone back into his pocket, he gazed at the wizard sidewise. "Okay, we're listening. What about my family, and what's it got to do with me?"

"That's a better attitude, Young Man. Now, let's discuss your father and you. Do you know what the seventh son of a seventh son is?"

"I think I heard that somewhere, but I don't know what it means." He turned to Jeremy who shrugged, and shook his head.

"Well, that's you, and it means your special. You're the seventh son of a seventh son, who is your father. That makes you different...important...to me, anyway."

Darren tilted his head. "Why?"

"First, let me dispense with this ridiculous wizard outfit I wore in your honor. I really thought you'd feel more comfortable around that character rather than anything else."

"Else, like what?"

He waved the wand in front of his face. The

uniform disappeared, replaced in a flash of amber light with matching black pants, shirt and a floor length cape. His countenance changed to reveal elongated incisors and deep set, red eyes. His fingernails grew to over two inches in length, curving under at the ends.

"Like a vampire."

Darren and Jeremy screamed in unison. Darren headed toward one of the exits, but the vampire dashed in front of him. Darren fell to the floor, immediately rolled to one side, and ran back toward Jeremy's chamber.

"What do you want, my blood?"

"Ha, ha. Not that simple. Sorry. If I only wanted blood, your brother would be a desiccated husk by now. No. I need your entire body...alive at first. So, I need your cooperation."

Darren shook uncontrollably. Tears coursed down his face. He collapsed to his knees.

"No."

"Oh, yes! You see, you were supposed to find my Conch shell first, but your brother disobeyed your parents, came out early, and found my invitation before you. By the way, Jeremy, that was very naughty of you."

"Let me go, and I promise I'll never disobey my parents again, ever." He began crying, and joined Darren on his knees.

"Again, not that simple for you either. I'm afraid you're going to regret touching my Conch." He strutted toward Darren who shifted to a seated position, and pushed himself hard against the chamber. "As to you, My Friend, we have much to discuss."

"Please, let us go. We won't tell anyone. We

promise."

Quinta ignored Darren's plea. He stood over him, allowing his drool to drip onto Darren's legs. Darren wiped off every drop, scrubbing his hands in the sand, hoping another disgusting drop wouldn't come; however, it did.

"Now, here's what's going to happen. This wand is special in our lives, Darren. Your great, great, great, great grandfather condemned me to this sandy grave many centuries ago when I attacked his sister. He had to destroy her, and blamed me for the whole affair. Foolish, wasn't he?"

Darren didn't respond. He couldn't respond. All he could do was whimper softly.

"Anyway, he then tricked me, and used the wand to confine me to this underworld. He was an extremely powerful wizard. This is his wand. I can do some neat tricks with it, but I can't do what he could. When he died, of natural causes, I might point out, I tricked one of his three sons into joining me here using a fancy gem as a lure. By the way, I knew you would respond better to a Conch shell than a gem, so I used that to attract you." He shrugged. "That son turned out to be a weak wizard. He had the wand with him, and tried to use it against me, but it didn't work. No power flowed through him, really. I easily took it from him, and then, I killed him."

Darren screamed at both the vision of his ancestor killed by this horrible creature, and what that might mean for him. Jeremy screamed in sympathy.

"I have been able to tunnel all over the world using the wand, but never upward. Don't know why. I suspect your ancestor condemned me using it, and somehow I can't use the same wand to escape. My only hope, I believe, is that a fully powerful wizard can dispel the curse that's keeping me here. That would be you, Seventh Son of the Seventh Son of an Ancient Wizard. Once I'm free, I'm afraid you will be of no further use to me. Now, do you understand?"

Darren nodded a few times, and then shook his head. He still couldn't utter a 'no.'

"Playing dumb, huh? Okay, I'll play your game. I've got all the time in the world anyway. You have inherited your ancestor's powers. There's something about that number of generations that changes your genes, allowing the powers hidden within them to emerge. So, presto, you're a wonderful wizard...at the age of twelve. You are twelve, aren't you? Turned twelve last week, a very long week for me indeed while I tunneled here to position myself under the beach. Twelve, right?"

Darren nodded, although he now wished he were eleven again.

"You're going to dispel this curse today. You're going to release me on humanity again, and the first thing I'm going to do is kill all your family members one-by-one, your brother there, your sister, your mother, and your father. Then, I'll hunt down all your aunts, uncles, and cousins. I'll have my revenge on your entire family. Your old ancestor thought he condemned me to a form of Hell forever, but I'll rise above him to prevail. It took me over a century to manufacture that gem, and another to form the Conch out of sand. He thought I couldn't figure a way out. I've even outsmarted him. I've won!"

Quinta threw his arms into the air, holding the wand far above his head.

An angry growl roared from behind Quinta. He turned, lowering the wand to use as a weapon, but moved too slowly. Birdie had charged him from one of the corridors, and flew at the vampire, catching his cape-covered arm. They fell to the ground. The wand flew into the air. Darren stretched toward the wand, but it flew beyond his reach, landing in the sand over twenty feet away.

As Darren crawled toward the wand, the vampire shook Birdie off his arm, tossing him against the wall. Birdie fell to the floor, coughed once, and, uninjured, bounded toward Darren. The vampire flew toward Darren, grabbed him by the scruff of his neck, and reached toward the wand.

"Come to Quinta, Wand."

"Fetch the stick, Birdie. Bring it to me. Fetch it, Boy." Darren pointed to the wand.

Birdie ran past Darren, but, before he could reach the wand, it shook, rose from the sand, and flew toward the vampire; however, it sailed by the vampire's outstretched hand, and slammed into Darren's.

The vampire howled at the disobedient wand, and yanked Darren higher into the air, reaching for his prize.

"No! It's my wand now!"

Quinta grabbed the wand, and screamed as a jolt of electricity blasted from the wand, and down his arm. The vampire released both Darren and the wand. Darren's eyes sprung open in surprise. He fell, but landed on his feet. He pointed the wand at the vampire, not knowing what he could possibly do, but realizing he had to try.

"Trap him in a force field like Jeremy."

The tip of the wand glowed red. A golden ray

sprang from its end, encircling the vampire several times before disappearing.

The vampire, still screeching, but realizing what had happened, pushed against the invisible force, but bounced off, falling against the other side before sliding to the floor.

Birdie stood by Darren, growling at the trapped vampire.

Darren reached down to pet Birdie's head. "Good boy! Did the mean vampire bite you?" Darren spent a full minute checking his friend for any signs of a bite, or scratch. He found none. "Good. Don't want a vampire dog for a pet."

"Don't forget me. I'm still trapped. Use that wand to release me. I want to go home."

Darren shrugged. "Don't really know how this thing works, but I'll give it a try." He pointed the wand at Jeremy. "Release Jeremy from the force field, but not the vampire. Please!"

A soft 'pop' accompanied a flash around Jeremy. Jeremy tested the wall of the force field with his hand. It easily passed through. He jumped into the air, smiling widely. "Hurrah, I'm free!" He glanced at the vampire, who now stood, trying every inch of his jail for any weakness. He found none.

"Which way out, Mister Vampire?"

The vampire growled his reply, jumping at the children as if no chamber existed. He bounced back, but the children recoiled. Birdie stood between the children and the vampire, and barked loudly at the vampire's attempted attack.

Darren turned his back on the vampire. "We've got to get out of here, but how?"

"Use your wand to make a tunnel up out of here."

Darren pointed the wand toward the ceiling.

"Make a tunnel home." Nothing.

"Ha, ha. I told you it wouldn't work upward. You're trapped in here with me forever, and, as soon as I figure a way out, I'm going to force you to dispel your ancestor's curse. Then, you're both dead."

Both boys backed away, turning toward the many corridors surrounding the clearing.

"Which way?"

Birdie barked, and ran into one corridor.

"Let's follow Birdie."

Birdie led them down several, branching corridors until they came to a dead end with the Conch shell in the sand.

"This is the spot." Darren picked up the Conch. "This is our ticket out. He pointed the wand at it. "Take us home to the beach."

The Conch rose, pulling Darren upward. Jeremy grabbed Birdie under his front legs, and held onto Darren as all three rose to the surface amid a red whirlpool of sand. They were ejected, falling to the sand just as the whirlpool sealed under them.

Birdie barked at the spot.

"What if the vampire got out of the force field now that the wand isn't down there anymore. Suppose he finds another way to come up here."

Darren spotted the Conch in the sand. A small whirlpool had started around it. "That Conch is the answer. If it opens a whirlpool to that underworld, he might be able to use it now to fly up here. We've got to destroy it."

Birdie growled at Darren, who turned toward the dog. Birdie held a stick the size of a baseball bat in his teeth. Darren grabbed it, petted Birdie once, and smashed the Conch. It exploded, sending bright red rays in all directions like a Fourth of July firework. The whirlpool ceased. Above their heads, the ominous clouds dissipated in an instant, allowing bright sunshine to warm the beach.

Jeremy shook his head. "No one is going to believe this."

"I don't think we should tell anyone. They'll think we're crazy, and we'll both be punished for... something. You know mom. Somehow it's always our fault."

"Yeah, you're right. What are you going to do about that wand?"

"It belongs to our family from way back. So, being the oldest, it's now mine. I guess I'll keep it. We may need it if that vampire ever gets out of the underground. He said it took over a century to whip up that Conch, so we should be safe for a while especially since he doesn't have this wand to work with." He studied the wand, waving it in the air. "But if anyone sees us use it, they'll probably take it away. I think we should hide it somewhere."

"Don't bury it. The vampire may dig around, and find it."

"Okay. We'll take it home, and hide it in our toy chest until we need it."

Birdie ran in circles around the boys, and then headed up the beach, looking back to ensure they followed. Both boys ran to keep up with Birdie, afraid they might lag behind, and fall victim to the vampire's teeth.

Darren risked a last look back. He swore he saw a cyclone of red sand where the Conch had exploded. He ran faster, grabbing Jeremy's hand as he passed, pulling him along. Spotting their yellow cottage in the distance, they breathed easier, but didn't slow their pace. Their mom awaited them on the front porch, smiling as they approached. Their father emerged from the water, joining them as they collapsed onto the beach.

"Racing up the beach?"

"Yeah, Dad. Birdie won. He's a great dog."

The father petted Birdie. "He should be for the price we paid for him. You know he's from a long line of vampire hunters, don't you."

Both boys froze, held their breaths, and stared at their father.

"What do you mean, Dad?"

"Well, the story goes that dogs from his family helped our wizard ancestors hunt vampires long ago. Eventually, those dogs were bred into the Black Labs of today. That's you, Birdie."

Birdie barked, and jumped against the father's chest.

"That wand you're hiding behind your back came from our ancestors, didn't it?"

"How did you know?"

"For generations, our family has been passing down the story of how one of ancestors imprisoned a vampire in the underworld. The wand he used disappeared from our care sometime after that. No one knew what had happened to it, although the rumor persisted that the vampire had somehow seized it. For generations, our kind could do no magic without it. Since it's in your hands, and neither of you appear hurt, I'd say you met this vampire, and took it away from him. Am I right."

"Kind of."

"Kind of?"

"Well, we couldn't have done it without Birdie. He got it away from the vampire, and led us through the corridors so we could get out. I used the wand to free Jeremy, and put the vampire in a force field, but Birdie's the real hero."

Jeremy could finally breathe easier. "You're not mad at us?"

Their mom approached the group. "Of course we're not mad at you. We knew it would happen someday. It had been predicted years ago that one of our family would have to confront that vampire to get the wand back. We didn't know exactly when that would happen, but we were sure that you, as the seventh son of the seventh son, would defeat him." She put her hands on her hips, and winked. "After all, you are our sons, and you have a great ancestry, and so does Birdie. That's why we've always had one of his breed as a pet. He's especially good at outsmarting vampires." She rubbed Birdie's neck, behind his ear. "Aren't you, Boy?"

Birdie barked, as he wagged his tail, and headed for the water.

"We're happy it's over. That's for sure." The father decided to join Birdie.

The mother waved at the duo headed for a swim. "That wand carries a lot of power with it, and a lot of responsibility, Darren. Jeremy, I'm afraid you'd have less success with it. So, you won't be able to use it."

"I don't want any part of it, especially if it means I may meet up with that vampire again. No, Darren, it's all yours!"

The mother smiled. "Don't worry, Jeremy, you have other talents you'll learn about later."

Darren examined his wand. "Are there other...talents, I think you called it, that I need to know about getting."

"Er...yes, but only when you're older. Don't worry about those now."

Jeremy chuckled. "Yeah, Darren, when you're an old man of thirteen."

Shaking water from his body, Birdie ran up to the group carrying a stick.

"That's the stick we found early this morning; isn't it, Birdie? Do you want me to throw it so you can fetch it?"

Instead of releasing the stick, Birdie, with tail wagging, knocked both boys down, dropped the stick between them, and licked their faces enthusiastically.

Laughter filled the beach.

***

You don't start out writing good stuff. You start out writing crap and thinking it's good stuff, and then you gradually get better at it. That's why I say one of the most valuable traits is persistence.

~ Octavia E Butler

Made in the USA
Middletown, DE
05 October 2021